"I need to

Jimmy grabbe   guided her back into
the bedroom. He pulled the door closed and locked
it behind them. "That won't hold them for long," he
said, tossing a blanket over the camera focused on
the crib.

Calvin stirred in Isobel's arms as he glanced up at
her with worried eyes.

Hands shaking, she jammed Calvin's favorite stuffie
next to her Bible in the side pocket of the backpack.
Across the room, Jimmy had pushed out the screen
of the double-hung window and was in the process
of disappearing through the opening.

Isobel blinked. Where was he going? Shouldn't he
stop and explain the plan?

A moment later, his head appeared, framed by the
window. "Hand me the kid," he said.

Still trembling, she set Calvin in his arms.

"Now you."

Her heart beating double time in her chest, she
straddled the sill and jumped.

Jimmy's countenance was calm and focused as he
returned Calvin to her arms. She pulled in a quick
breath of relief. Jimmy was a trained marshal. He
knew what he was doing. He would protect her and
her son...

Jaycee Bullard was born and raised in the great state of Minnesota, the fourth child in a family of five. Growing up, she loved to read, especially books by Astrid Lindgren and Georgette Heyer. In the ten years since graduating with a degree in classical languages, she has worked as a paralegal and an office manager, before finally finding her true calling as a preschool Montessori teacher and as a writer of romantic suspense.

Books by Jaycee Bullard

Love Inspired Suspense

Framed for Christmas
Fatal Ranch Reunion
Rescue on the Run
Cold Case Contraband
Protecting the Littlest Witness
Under the Marshal's Watch

Visit the Author Profile page at LoveInspired.com.

UNDER THE MARSHAL'S WATCH

JAYCEE BULLARD

LOVE INSPIRED SUSPENSE
INSPIRATIONAL ROMANCE

LOVE INSPIRED® SUSPENSE
INSPIRATIONAL ROMANCE

Recycling programs
for this product may
not exist in your area.

ISBN-13: 978-1-335-95717-7

Under the Marshal's Watch

Copyright © 2025 by Jean Bullard

For questions and comments about the quality of this book, please contact us at CustomerService@Harlequin.com.

® is a trademark of Harlequin Enterprises ULC.

Love Inspired
22 Adelaide St. West, 41st Floor
Toronto, Ontario M5H 4E3, Canada
www.LoveInspired.com

Printed in Lithuania

MIX
Paper | Supporting
responsible forestry
FSC® C021394

Have mercy upon me, O God, according to thy lovingkindness: according unto the multitude of thy tender mercies blot out my transgressions.
—*Psalm* 51:1

To my brother-in-law Paul.

And to Daisy and Danny, the two newest littles.

ONE

As she did every morning before coffee and toast, Isobel Carrolls took out a Sharpie and drew an *X* on the calendar hanging on the kitchen wall. Forty-one days down, and three to go until the trial.

It had been almost six weeks of waiting and worrying, but how could she complain? Her ex-husband, Ricky, was in jail. And she was alive, and so was her nine-month-old son, Calvin. Still, she had to wonder how her life had gotten so far off course since that snowy day last winter when Ricky was arrested for attempted kidnapping and murder in Dagger Lake. That had seemed the end of it then or, at the very least, the beginning of the end. But she should never have let herself to hope. Sure enough, the feds pulled rank, postponing the state proceedings to go after Ricky for more wide-ranging crimes—racketeering, extortion and money laundering—in upcoming hearings that would take place in Detroit. And when other witnesses for the prosecution began to mysteriously disappear, she and Calvin were abruptly relocated to a safe house in northern Minnesota.

Isobel's first look at the primitive log cabin set back on an overgrown lot had done little to put her mind at ease. But the place had all the modern conveniences of home—a dishwasher, washer and dryer, cable TV. And, best of all, twelve state-of-the-art cameras monitoring the property and four federal marshals providing on-site protection twenty-four hours a day. It was a life with many restrictions and few responsibilities—but those responsibilities were due to ramp up, starting today.

She pulled out a chair and took a seat at the kitchen table. Across from her sat Deputy US Marshals Len Roth and Meredith Strong, the "A" team as they had dubbed themselves in a nod to their combined forty years of experience compared to the much younger duo of Jimmy Flynn and Ryan Peterson, who worked the day shift from ten to ten. Joining them this morning was Stephanie Marsh, one of the prosecutors assigned to the case. According to Meredith, Stephanie was a rock star in the US Attorney's Office in Detroit, with a number of big wins in the high-profile assignments that had crossed her desk. Isobel could only hope that Stephanie and the rest of the team had equal success in going up against Ricky.

Coffee cups were shifted to make room for documents and scribbled notes as Stephanie began with an apologetic smile. "Yesterday was just for gathering background information that might be relevant to the trial. Today we get down to brass tacks. How about we start with a few softball questions you'll be asked right off the bat when you take the stand?"

Isobel nodded. She was ready for the easy stuff.

"The first thing I'll do is ask you to state your full name, address and occupation."

"Isobel Carrolls, 356 Dunwoody Drive, Apartment 2A, Dagger Lake, North Dakota. Oh, and I work as a bank teller, though I'm currently on leave because of threats made against me before trial."

A pained expression washed over Stephanie's face. "Remember what we talked about yesterday, Isobel. We're going to hold back on that kind of information in the initial part of your testimony. It'll have a stronger impact if it comes out organically." She looked down at the prep sheet in front of her and continued. "Next, you'll be asked to describe your relationship to the defendant."

Ugh. Isobel suppressed a small shiver. The thought of discussing her marriage in front of a courtroom of spectators was one of the things she had been dreading most.

"Can't she just say that she never had a clue that her husband would turn out to be a deranged killer who would try to blow her up at the bank and kidnap her baby?" Len Roth smirked.

Stephanie shook her head. "I told you before, and I'll say it again. We show, we don't just tell, Len."

Show, don't tell. Isobel pinched her lips together in a frown. She understood what was being asked of her, but she was finding it difficult to relate to the mindset of her twenty-two-year-old self. Innocent, naïve and trusting. Not so much anymore. Living with a man who had little respect for human life had changed her. She had grown up during her marriage. She was no longer the blithely self-centered bride who was worried that her wedding cake was only two tiers instead of three. No, now she was always on guard, watching over her shoulder, ever vigilant to any possible threat against Calvin.

Stephanie pulled in a long breath. "Don't sweat the small stuff, Isobel. That's why I'm here. To prep you for those kinds of questions." She paused as a plaintive wail was amplified through the kitchen.

Isobel's eyes went to the monitor on the counter with feeds from the twelve cameras inside and outside the cabin.

In the one at the bottom, focused on Calvin's crib, she could see that the little boy had pulled himself upright and was making his dismay clear with a full-throated scream.

"Sounds like someone wants us to know he's up and ready for the day." Meredith Strong laughed. "Why don't I get him and bring him into the kitchen?"

"Thanks, Meredith, but I'll do it. I won't take the time to nurse this morning, so I'll just heat up some formula before I bring him into the kitchen." Isobel moved across the room, took the bottle from the refrigerator and placed it in the warmer.

A moment later, the green light blinked, indicating that the liquid had reached optimal temperature. "Back in a flash," Isobel said. She grabbed the dripping bottle and headed to the bedroom down the hall.

Calvin stopped yelping the minute she entered the room.

"Good morning, sweet pea." She lifted her little boy into her arms, allowing him to nestle against her shoulder, tempted as always to prolong what had become her favorite part of the day. But Stephanie was waiting with all her lists and her piles of paperwork, so she quickened her pace. Once Calvin's diaper was changed, she selected a soft blue one-piece romper to replace his jammies, noting that he looked more babyish than ever with his bare, chubby legs kicking high in the air. Tucking his bottle into her backpack with the rest of her gear, she headed into the hall, almost colliding with the solid six-foot frame of Jimmy Flynn.

"I didn't expect to see you this early, Marshal Flynn," she said. "Is Ryan here, too?"

Jimmy wiped his fingers on a wad of paper towels he had tucked under his arm. "I assume he's still back at the bunk house. I thought I'd get a head start on unclogging that dodgy drain so the little guy can have his morning bath."

Leave it to Jimmy to notice a problem and set about fixing it. Kind. That was the word to describe him. Kind *and* dependable. But good deeds were not on the docket this morning. Isobel turned to face him with an apologetic frown. "I appreciate your thoughtfulness. But Calvin's bath can wait until tonight. Stephanie's anxious to get started on the trial prep."

Crash! Bang! Bang! Bang!

Gunfire. She recognized the sound immediately. A gasp stuck in her throat as Jimmy stepped forward to shield her body with his.

"Who? What?" she asked, her voice quaking. But she knew the answer. Ricky's men had found them.

"Security has been breeched. I need to get you out of here." Jimmy grabbed her arm and guided her back into the bedroom. He pulled the door closed and locked it behind them. "That won't hold them for long," he said, tossing a blanket over the camera focused on the crib.

Calvin stirred in Isobel's arms as he glanced up at her with worried eyes. "It's okay," she whispered as she smoothed his soft downy hair. But it didn't feel okay. It felt like the end of the world.

Hands shaking, she jammed Bingo, Calvin's favorite stuffie, next to her Bible in the side pocket of the backpack. Across the room, having pushed out the screen of the double-hung window, Jimmy was in the process of disappearing through the opening.

Isobel blinked. Where was he going? Shouldn't he stop and explain the plan?

A moment later, his head appeared, framed by the window. "Hand me the kid," he said.

Still trembling, she set Calvin in his arms.

"Now you."

Her heart beating double-time in her chest, she straddled the sill and jumped.

Her feet had barely touched the ground when Jimmy reached into the bag dangling from her shoulder. He pulled out Calvin's plastic giraffe and tossed it toward a stand of evergreens at the edge of the property.

"Here's hoping they'll assume we ran in that direction."

"But won't they return when they discover we're not there?" Cold, clammy fear squeezed at her heart.

"Eventually. But not right away."

Jimmy's countenance was calm and focused as he returned Calvin to her arms. She pulled in a quick breath of relief. Jimmy was a trained marshal. He knew what he was doing. He would protect her and her son.

Jimmy dropped to his knees and peeled back a piece of the lattice strip covering the crawl space under the house.

"Think you can you slide in there on your stomach?"

She nodded. It was tight, with only about a foot of clearance between the subfloor and the ground, but she was certain she could fit into the space.

"Good. Hand the baby and the backpack to me. When you're situated, I'll pass them through the opening."

Isobel did as she was asked and then stretched out on the ground and shimmied into the space. The scent of mold and dry dirt assailed her nostrils, along with something else, too—rotting leaves? Or worse, maybe the corpse of some animal that had gotten trapped under the house and couldn't get out? She could deal with the smell. Harder to ignore was the relentless pounding in the floorboards above her as the intruders hammered against the locked door.

"Any minute, they're going to break the lock and get into the room." Her voice shook as panic coursed through her senses.

"We have time. Ready?" Jimmy reached through the opening and set Calvin into Isobel's outstretched arms.

"Got him," she said.

"And here. You might need this," he said as he slipped her backpack next to her on the ground.

Good point. She reached into the front pouch and pulled out the bottle, which she tilted sideways for Calvin to drink.

"Jimmy?" she said, startled to hear his name on her lips. For weeks, she had referred to him as Marshal Flynn. But somehow that no longer seemed appropriate. "Aren't you going to join us?"

She could see his eyes, dark and thoughtful, mulling over the question. Was he thinking of taking on the shooters directly? How was that going to work, since she had noticed right away that his shoulder holster was empty?

The floorboards above them rumbled with the crack of wood flying off the hinges. Jimmy seemed to take that as his cue to back into the narrow crawl space, quickly pushing the sagging lattice back into place.

Not a moment too soon. Heavy footsteps pounded across the floor above them, followed by the thump of boots landing on the ground next to the window.

"Where'd she go?" a gruff voice demanded.

"Not sure," a second man answered. "But wherever she went, she won't get far, not if she's carrying the kid."

"She could be hiding in the bushes," the first man said. "Maybe we should scout the perimeter."

Scout the perimeter? Isobel's heart somersaulted in her chest. Clearly, it was only a matter of time before one of them discovered their hiding place under the house.

Peering through the lattice covering, Jimmy Flynn could see the boots of two men planted on the ground inches from the house. Clearly, this was not an optimal situation. He and Isobel were sitting ducks, crammed into an uncomfortably small space with a nine-month-old baby who might at any moment decide that he'd rather cry than drink his bottle. But however vulnerable their present position, hiding had seemed like the best choice two minutes earlier when he'd noticed the crawl space under the house.

Now he wasn't so sure. Maybe it would have been a better call to make a run for his van in the driveway of the bunkhouse where he and Ryan stayed between shifts. But that would have required them to cover roughly the length of a football field with a baby in their arms, and he couldn't take that chance. And heading for the wooded area in the back of the cabin had seemed equally perilous with their pursuers so close behind. In any case, it was too late to change course now.

If only he hadn't lightened his belt when he'd stooped to plunge out the bathtub drain, setting his cell on the shelf and his gun into a basket under the sink. With the witness's life at stake, any attempt to retrieve either item at the sound of the first shots would have been a risky move, one that, even if successful, would have used up precious seconds in their escape. His fingers clenched as he thought about his SIG. It would come in handy right now as the men outside were dangerously close to discovering their hiding place.

Or not. One of the intruders suddenly shifted his stance and headed away from the cabin.

Jimmy held his breath and waited.

A moment passed and the man returned to rejoin his companion.

"Look what I found in the grass! The kid must have dropped it when they ran toward the woods. Now that we know which way they're headed, finding them will be a piece of cake. The others are inside dealing with the bodies, so they'll be here if the woman doubles back and returns to the house."

Again, Jimmy waited and watched as the two sets of boots disappeared into the distance.

He counted off the seconds in his head. Seventy-four, seventy-five...the coast ought to be clear, at least for the moment.

"I think they're gone." He turned to face Isobel, who had slung an arm around Calvin as she'd curled up on her side.

"Should we check and see if Len and Meredith need help?" she whispered.

Jimmy pulled in a deep breath. He had been trying not to think about the likely fate of his fellow marshals.

"No. These guys are pros. They shoot to kill. They wouldn't have left any witnesses."

"Stephanie, too?"

Jimmy nodded.

"But how did they find us? Meredith said that our location was top secret, restricted to a handful of people with a need to know."

That was true. The details involving the safe house had been arranged with great care, recognizing all contingencies. And everyone involved in the protective unit had all been vetted with the utmost care. The four marshals, their boss at headquarters and even Stephanie, an assistant US attorney for the State of Michigan, had passed muster. Someone must have flipped and revealed their location. But who?

Len? Nah. Len was a by-the-book old-timer, canny and spry despite his fifty years. Then again, he was five years away from a much-anticipated early retirement. A big cash payday would go a long way toward the purchase of that condo in Florida that he loved to talk about between shifts.

Meredith? Jimmy had recognized almost immediately that her easygoing manner hid the fact that she was ambitious and focused—and maybe still bitter about being passed over for that last promotion. And Stephanie, who had just arrived a day earlier to begin the trial prep, was an even more unlikely culprit behind the betrayal. Unless, of course, she had been followed on her drive from the airport. The fact was that the mole could have been anyone. And even if there was someone still alive in the kitchen, it was too risky to go back and check the body count.

Isobel propped her chin up with her arm and turned to face him. "Do you think someone slipped up and accidentally mentioned something about our location?"

Jimmy shook his head. "That's not supposed to happen."

"But." Isobel looked aghast. "That means that whoever did this signed a death warrant for the others. And what about Ryan? What's going to happen when he shows up for his shift?"

Good question. The raid had taken place when both he and his partner were supposed to be off duty, which seemed like more than an odd coincidence.

Still, he didn't like thinking Ryan was the mole. He hadn't known the man for long, but he had gotten a good read on his new partner in the time they had worked together. Yet he also knew that no one was completely incorruptible. Even someone known and trusted was capable of duplicity and betrayal. Especially when given an incentive. Isobel's ex-husband was a desperate man facing a life sentence without parole. A desperate man with money and power had the means to flip even the most dedicated agent.

The how and the why security had been breached were questions for another day. Bottom line—Calvin and Isobel were his responsibility. He snuck a glance at the woman stretched out next to him in the crawl space. Her dark brown hair hanging down in loose curls framed a heart-shaped face that could only be described as beautiful. Add in a pair of deep brown eyes etched with vulnerability and he recognized the allure someone like that would have to a man like Ricky. But Isobel hadn't been the wide-eyed innocent of a dark fairy tale either. She had stayed married to Ricky for three years, been privy to at least some of his secrets and done nothing to expose them. Only after he had tried to kidnap their son had she stepped forward to testify against him.

Jimmy shook his head. It was not up to him to judge. His only job was to protect the lives of the witness and her son.

But for some reason, this particular mission felt a lot more personal. Isobel's optimistic spirit seemed to permeate everything she did, from her thoughtful interactions with the other agents to the tender way she cared for her little boy. Despite the bad choices that had led her to this place, she deserved a break, and he had resolved to do everything in his power to make sure she got one.

He moved a few inches forward and pressed his face against the opening.

There was no sign of the gunmen.

This could be his only opportunity to sneak inside the house to get his weapon. Of course, that would mean leaving Isobel and the baby defenseless while he did so. But he couldn't see that he had much choice.

He turned to face Isobel.

"I'm thinking that making a run for the van is our best chance to get out of here alive. But to do that, I'm going to need my gun. I'm going to have to go inside to get it."

"Okay." She offered him a tentative smile. No questions,

no complaints. She put on a brave face in spite of the danger, he'd give her that.

"Good. I'll be back in five minutes, maybe less." He gave Isobel a thumbs-up and then turned and pushed aside the lattice strip covering the crawl space.

"Godspeed," she whispered.

He inched forward into the opening. When he made it through, he turned to tuck the strip back in place.

It took a few seconds for his eyes to adjust to the light as he scanned the area around the house. Two of the men seemed to have disappeared into the trees at the back of the property. But there would be several others inside the house. He pulled himself up on the window ledge, swung around and entered the bedroom. Only a few more feet to cover and he'd reach the hall. A half dozen more steps and he'd be inside the bathroom where he'd left his gun.

He had made it to the doorway when a trill of music stopped him in his tracks.

Unless one of the gunmen had "Should've Been a Cowboy" as his ringtone, someone was calling his phone.

TWO

Jimmy plastered his body against the wall and waited, willing the caller to give up after one ring. The cell trilled again. He pulled in a long breath and held it until the notes stopped playing.

"That was definitely a phone," a voice boomed through the silence. "It sounded like it was coming from somewhere down the hall. Maybe it belongs to the witness, though I doubt it. The feds wouldn't have let her bring it along while waiting for trial."

True enough. Isobel's phone and her tablet had been left behind at her place in Dagger Lake. Jimmy remembered being impressed that she hadn't protested or complained about relinquishing all forms of contact with the outside world.

"You check the bathroom, Matt." The man issuing orders was clearly in charge. "I'll head into the bedroom and see what I can find."

Jimmy took a nosedive under the bed seconds before the intruder entered the room. He shimmied backward as far as he could, tensing as he waited, knowing his hiding place would be discovered the moment the man bent down to look for the phone.

But there didn't seem to be much searching going on.

The bedsprings creaked. The mattress sagged as another phone trilled and a gruff voice above him was quick to answer.

"Yeah. The doctored feed on the CCTV did give us the element of surprise, but the girl wasn't in the kitchen. She escaped through the bedroom window with the kid…Yeah, I know. We'll keep looking. She's got to be somewhere, right?"

Long pause.

"Wait. What?…Yeah, the kid's okay. Didn't you hear me? Listen. I'm going to need to call you back from a different spot. My cell keeps cutting out midsentence."

The thump of boots signaled someone entering the room.

"I found the phone," a man with a deep voice said. "But it's locked."

"We can check it out later. Matt. Priority one right now is to take out the witness. It will be a real problem if she gets away."

"She won't. Dez left a few minutes ago to join the search, and I'm headed outside to see if they missed something. Maybe I'll find her hiding in the shed."

"Let's hope so, for all of our sakes. I need to call the boss back and make sure he has every angle covered if she does manage to get away."

The bedsprings groaned again, followed by a shuffling of footsteps across the floor. Jimmy slid forward toward the edge of the bed and waited until it felt safe to come out.

Impatience gnawed at his gut. He needed to do something before one of the gunmen noticed the crawl space under the house.

He pulled himself upright and headed across the room, pressing his body against the doorframe for a view of the hall. A man's back was to him as he paced the length of the corridor, phone in one hand, Luger in the other. Even from the back, Jimmy recognized the shiny bald head and stocky build of a man he had seen in photos in the file. He was Josh Capon, one of Ricky's chief lieutenants. Capon had to know that if this operation went wrong, there would be no second chances. He and his team would suffer immediate repercussions. Ricky Bashir was a hardened criminal who had no patience with associates who failed to make problems go away. No wonder Capon was desperate to find the witness and make things right.

Jimmy leaned closer, hoping to hear something to clue him in to the identity of the mole. But the person on the other end of the line seemed to be doing most of the talking, with Capon doing all of the listening as he paced the hall. Three steps forward, a half turn and then three steps back, his fingers lingering close to the trigger. No way could Jimmy make it into the bathroom without being spotted. Or into the kitchen to assess the scene.

New plan. But he'd need to act fast. He headed across the room toward the window, checked to make sure the coast was clear and then jumped onto the lawn, relieved to see that the lattice covering the crawl space was still in place.

Another positive—the men didn't seem to suspect that he'd been present in the house at the time of the raid. That would allow for the element of surprise when he made his next move.

Now all he had to do was find a shrub along the property leafy enough to provide cover as he waited for the man called Matt to begin his search.

How long had Jimmy been gone? Ten minutes? Twenty? For Isobel, it felt like an eternity spent staring at Calvin and willing him not to cry. For the first time ever, she was grateful that she had already started to wean him onto the bottle. At the moment at least, her son was happily drinking his formula, stopping occasionally to shoot her one of his perfect smiles.

Her beautiful boy. Waiting for that smile was almost enough distraction to keep her from thinking about all the bad choices leading to this point in her life.

Almost, but not quite, as regrets and recriminations flooded her brain. She could never really explain why she had gotten tangled up with Ricky Bashir in the first place. She'd been so foolish, so blind, so young and trusting. If only she had been smarter, with more self-confidence, she could have spurred his advances and tried to make it on her own. But that line of thinking was a rabbit hole, and she couldn't let herself go down it again. Too much of her recent past had been spent questioning her reasons for marrying such a cruel, bitter man. That she had jumped into that relationship with open eyes, never questioning the story Ricky had spun about his past, was a shame she would carry for the rest of her life.

Of course, she had her excuses. Ricky had swept her off her feet, lavishing her with gifts and attention and promises about a shining future together.

Countless conversations with her best friend, Abby, had gotten her no closer to understanding why she hadn't acted sooner in leaving Ricky. Maybe testifying in court would give her the closure she needed to move on, if only she could stay strong under cross-examination. But forgiving herself would be even harder to do now that her attorney and two federal agents were dead.

The floorboards above her creaked and she scooted a few inches closer to Cal. If only she knew what was happening in the room above her; if only she had eyes on Marshal

Jimmy Flynn. Instead, she was stuck here, inches from—a gasp stuck in her throat—a hideously large spider and several eviscerated insects stuck to a wispy web stretched across the planks above her head. Her old self—the posh, high-maintenance woman she had been when she was married to Ricky—would have been brought to tears by such a predicament. But she had left that person behind when she'd moved to Dagger Lake. A huge spider had nothing on her ex-husband and his associates when it came to causing paralyzing fright to course through her veins.

And horrible as Ricky was, she could never forget the one good thing that had come from her marriage. She cast her eyes sideways at her little son, who once again decided to grace her with a toothy grin.

The innocence of babes.

In the year that had passed since she had broken free of Ricky's web, she had learned a lot about being brave. And how to love completely. And now both of those new emotions had merged into a fierce desire to protect her son and keep him safe from her ex-husband, who appeared to be calling the shots from jail.

She scooted forward and tried to peek through the lattice covering. How could a simple trip to retrieve a weapon be taking this long? Unless… She hesitated to even think about what might have happened if Jimmy had been caught inside the house.

At least she hadn't heard a shot. That was good, wasn't it? All she could do now was keep praying and begging God to keep him safe.

"Psst! Isobel!"

Jimmy! Relief swamped her senses. She blinked as the

lattice was pulled back and the marshal's face appeared in the opening.

"You okay?" she said.

"Fine. Ready to go?"

He didn't need to ask twice. She lifted Calvin and handed him up to Jimmy. Then she took hold of his outstretched hand and pulled herself upright.

She followed Jimmy toward a cluster of bushes at the front of the house, stumbling as she tripped over a body lying on the ground.

"Who…?"

"His name's Matt, I think. I had to knock him out to get his gun." He reached into his pocket and pulled out a set of keys. "Take these. When I say go, head across the lawn toward the bunkhouse. It'll be a hundred-yard dash, give or take a few feet. But don't think about the distance or what's going on around you. Just focus on running as fast as you can."

She could do that. Back in high school, she'd been a pretty decent sprinter. Of course, she'd never run a race carrying a baby. Or on terrain this uneven and dotted with rocks. Her gaze scraped the open space stretched in front of them. She had asked about why the cabin was so isolated, and one of the agents—Ryan maybe?—had said that the privacy it offered from passersby was one of the draws in choosing the place. Apparently, that hadn't been enough to keep them safe.

"What about you?" she asked.

"I'll be right behind you. If Ryan's around, he'll provide backup. He usually goes out on a run around this time, so I'm not banking on his help. You'd be faster without the kid, but he's safer with you. And remember. If I go down, you get in the van and start driving. Follow the signs into town."

"But…"

"No time for questions. Ready? Go."

With Calvin clinging to her arms, she took off running.

She had covered less than fifty feet when she caught a glimpse of Jimmy. He was just a yard or two behind her, gun in his hand and his head turned sideways.

Pop! Pop!

And then: *Bang! Bang!* The noise was closer now: Jimmy returning fire at their pursuers.

"Time to turn on the gas." She imagined her mother's version of an inspirational cheer shouted from the sidelines during a track meet. It had never caused her to go any faster. She was already moving as quickly as she could. Still, it didn't hurt to know that someone had cared.

Well, Jimmy cared if she made it to the van. And so had Stephanie and all the federal marshals who had given their lives so that justice would be served. Isobel wanted that, too, but the most important thing at the moment was not how much anyone cared.

She was running for Calvin. Everything she did, she did for him.

Ahead, in the distance, was the small bunkhouse. In the driveway, Jimmy's blue van. She was ten yards away, but her legs felt like jelly and her body ached from the weight of the fifteen-pound baby in her arms.

Pop! Pop! She looped an arm around Calvin's head and pulled him closer to her chest as protection against any stray bullet that might come his way. The rhythm of her footsteps kept time to the beat playing in her head. *Turn on the gas. Turn on the gas.* She swiveled sideways to check on Jimmy. He had dropped back behind a tree, pinned down by their pursuers.

She blinked once as a familiar shape could be seen in

the distance. Ryan, clad head-to-toe in exercise gear, seemingly frozen in place in front of the bunkhouse. He seemed to be slowly taking in the scene around him before pulling a gun from the waistband of his sweatpants and then firing a round in the direction of Jimmy's pursuers.

Isobel reached the van first, panting, frantically pressing the key fob. Were the doors even locked? It didn't matter. The important thing was that the sliding door swooshed open. She set Calvin down into the car seat and tumbled onto the floor.

A bullet shattered the side window as Jimmy flung himself into the front and Ryan landed with a thud next to her in the back. The back door slid closed. Shots pinged against the doors on the side of the van and she covered Calvin as best she could. Then they were moving, swirling up thick clouds of dust as they pulled away from the curb.

When Jimmy and Ryan had first picked her up in Dagger Lake, she'd been surprised that a federal agent would choose to drive a minivan, especially since even she, being an actual mom, would not select that particular vehicle if given a choice. But during the course of the trip to the safe house, she had come to appreciate the van's advantages, especially its sliding door that made it easy to get Calvin in and out of his car seat. The vehicle was certainly a refuge now.

The more she thought about Marshal Jimmy Flynn, the more he seemed like a minivan type of guy. Solid. Professional. Good in a crisis. Maybe he was married and had a kid of his own, though he had never mentioned it. Then again, he didn't talk much about his personal life, so anything was possible.

"What's happening?" Ryan had to raise his voice to be heard over Calvin's wails.

"They found the safe house," Jimmy called back.

"How?"

"I don't know."

"There had to be a mole. Do you think it was Len?"

"What?" All Jimmy's frustration seemed captured in that single word.

"Len," Ryan repeated. "He's the obvious choice, don't you agree? Hey! Watch it!" Ryan shouted, pointing to the left. "You'll miss the turn,"

Jimmy twisted the wheel and the van overcorrected, skidding onto the shoulder. Gravel flew, pebbles shooting in every direction as he fought to wrestle the vehicle back into the lane.

Isobel held her breath as tension pulsed all around her. She forced her focus on Calvin, who was arching his back and slowly sliding out of his car seat. She swiveled sideways toward Ryan. "Help me, please. He's kicking so much that I can't clip the lock." There hadn't been time to buckle him in before.

Ryan put his gun down on the seat and gripped the baby's legs while Isobel fumbled with the mechanism. She almost had it clicked into place when the van careened into another turn.

A second hard push and the lock engaged. But Isobel's relief was short-lived as Jimmy turned sideways and she caught a hint of panic on his face.

"Do you have your phone?" Jimmy's voice cracked with desperation as his eyes locked on Ryan, who was bent on his hands and knees on the floor.

"It fell out of my pocket when I jumped into the van."

"What about your gun?"

"It slid under the seat." Ryan stretched his arm out, searching for it. "I'm trying to reach it but it seems to be stuck."

"We need to be ready because it won't be long before they're behind us. Did you see those two black Suburbans parked a quarter mile from the safe house along the frontage road? They have to belong to the intruders, don't you think? And they're packing some major muscle. I recognized Josh Capon, one of Bashir's main lieutenants."

Isobel bit back a gasp at Jimmy's next words.

"I heard them say they want the kid. And that can't happen until the rest of us are dead."

THREE

Jimmy pushed his foot down harder on the accelerator, desperate to put as many miles as possible between the van and their pursuers as cornfields, their stubby stalks abandoned in the harvest, stretched as far as the eye could see along the narrow two-lane road.

"Did you find your gun?" Jimmy addressed his question to Ryan, who was wedged in the back on bended knees.

"I see it, but I can't pry it free from the metal bars under the seat."

Great. Now there was a loaded pistol somewhere on the floor. Jimmy took a long, deep breath. While it was true that Ryan had eventually provided backup during the attack, why had it taken him so long to react to the threat? Why hadn't he heard the shots and investigated right away?

And what about Ryan's declaration that Len was the mole without any evidence to prove it? Was it an attempt to deflect blame? In any case, how could Ryan know anything for sure? Jimmy sure didn't. All he could testify to was hearing a spray of bullets and the thudding sounds of bodies hitting the floor.

Was it possible that their betrayer was someone higher up in the marshals? Jimmy thought about the conversation he had overheard while he was under the bed. The team that had attacked the safe house must have known the location of the security cameras and the layout of the cabin, which would seem to eliminate a number of people from the mix.

"Who gave us up, Jimmy?" Ryan seemed to read his mind even as he continued his efforts to retrieve his gun.

"I wish I knew. But I don't have a clue about what happened or how we were found. Or even who was killed. And I don't have a plan at the moment besides getting away." He checked the mirror again. He'd feel better once they reached the county highway. Right now, theirs was the only vehicle on the road, which made them sitting ducks should the perps catch up to them. On the plus side, the van was showing surprisingly good speed. Maybe, just maybe, they could outrun their pursuers.

"I don't get it. How could they have gotten past the cameras? How was it possible that no one had the chance to pull a gun?" Ryan seemed angered by the lack of ready answers to his questions.

Jimmy blew out a sigh. He needed to focus on driving. Not that his mind wasn't working itself into knots with those same thoughts. But still, having a shouted conversation about how much they didn't understand didn't seem like a good idea. Isobel had finally gotten Calvin quieted down, but she wasn't offering any insights of her own. He glanced at her in the rearview mirror. She had to have heard what he had said earlier about the men wanting to kidnap her son. It was a nightmare she had lived through once already, and it seemed supremely unfair that she should be going through the same thing a second time.

Of course, the men wanted to take Isobel out as well. She was a smart woman, and she knew that, too. At the moment, one of her hands was clutching Calvin's pudgy fingers between her own and the other was balled up into a fist and pressed against her chest. Her eyes were closed, but her lips seemed to be forming soundless words. Maybe she was praying. Well, that couldn't hurt, right?

But Jimmy wasn't about to put his trust into some invisible entity who seemed to run the world with an arbitrary randomness. But if there ever was a time to appeal to a higher power, this was probably as good as any.

Or maybe Isobel was going into shock. It wasn't an impossible thought considering the events of the past hour.

"Isobel? Everything good back there?"

A slight nod of the chin was the only indication she'd heard his question.

"Ryan!" His voice must have had a sharper edge than he realized as his other agent's head popped up to alert. "Will you check Isobel and the baby make sure they're okay?"

Jimmy watched in the mirror as Ryan pulled himself up onto the back seat.

"All good," Isobel interrupted before Ryan could take her pulse. Her voice was quiet but strong, no wobble or hysterical tinge. "All good," she repeated as she unfurled her fisted fingers and wiped them against her eyes.

A renewed determination wound through Jimmy's chest. There would be time enough to assign blame for what had happened once the witness was safe. But as much as he wanted to offer reassurance that everything was going to be okay, he also knew that a such claim was baseless in this moment. And he wasn't about to give false hope. He hated false hope. And he had way too much respect for Isobel to mislead her.

"Look, I can't say for sure that we're in the clear, but it's a good sign that there's no one following us. Just keep calm and carry on, right?"

"Keep calm and carry on?" Ryan repeated his words

with a definite touch of derision. "This isn't time for platitudes. It's time for action. For brainstorming. And I still want to know what happened back at the house. What were *you* doing there?"

Jimmy could feel his shoulders tighten. Was it his imagination or was there more than a hint of accusation in Ryan's voice?

"I was unplugging the drain in the tub while you were out on a run. Neither of us is to blame for what happened, okay? But you want to talk about solutions. Fine. What do you think we should do next?"

"I say we get local law enforcement involved. Better yet, find a phone and check in with the field offices. I know there's a tendency is go all lone wolf on this, but I suspect there are better solutions."

Jimmy couldn't hold back the scoff that escaped his throat. "C'mon, Ryan. Think about it. At least four gunmen, maybe more, broke into our supposedly secret safe house and shot two marshals and a federal attorney. The men who did this are determined to stop us at all costs." Jimmy knew that he was going too far, especially when Isobel choked out a gasp of dismay, but he needed to drive his point home. "I've read the file. You've read the file. Ricky Bashir planned a bank heist to kidnap his child. We have evidence that his people attempted to bribe officials in Michigan and North Dakota. He'll have backup and contingency plans. And until we know more, we shouldn't trust anyone."

Isobel shivered in her seat. She didn't want to agree with Jimmy Flynn. She wanted to jump on board with the idea that there were solutions other than just running away. She was tired of running away. But Jimmy was right. Ricky was ruthless. And smart. And manipulative. Once again, he had ordered the kill without any regard for innocent life. If Calvin hadn't woken early and Jimmy hadn't come to fix the tub, his plan would have been successful. It wasn't chance. It had been through the grace of God.

The tears that had been prickling the backs of her eyes leaked out, but she quickly brushed them away. She didn't need to add to the agents' burden by showing fear and weakness.

After their heated debate, the two men had lapsed into an uneasy silence. She couldn't quite see Jimmy's face as he drove at what felt like a reckless speed up and down the rolling hills, but he managed to convey an absolute confidence and control. His jaw was clenched and his arms holding the steering wheel looked poised for action.

Ryan, meanwhile, was still jostling around on the floor. She supposed she should be more concerned about the fact that his loaded gun was stuck under the seat, but it seemed to be the least of their problems. Actually, she felt sorry for Ryan. Jimmy's voice had been sharp, and the facts he'd laid out brokered no argument. Ryan had only been trying to brainstorm ideas. But the fact remained that Jimmy was right.

She sighed and squeezed Calvin's hand once again. It all felt so hopeless. If Ricky could find them at the safe house, he could find them anywhere. One step forward, two steps back. But no, that wasn't fair. Two steps forward, one step back. Calvin was still in her care. And she was still alive and ready to testify against Ricky.

"Uh, Jimmy?" Ryan's voice finally broke the silence.

"Yeah, yeah, yeah. I see it." Jimmy's voice was quieter now but still laced with determination.

Isobel turned her head and her heart dropped. The thread

of hope coiled in her chest snapped. Still a distance behind them, two identical black SUVs had appeared on the road. And they were getting closer every second.

"Maybe it's not them," she ventured.

"It's definitely them." Jimmy's tone was flat and certain.

Of course, he was right. Of course, it had to be Ricky's men. But how? She turned her head to look at Ryan. Through narrowed eyes, he seemed to be keeping a sharp watch on what was happening in the road behind them.

The silence that followed was unnerving. Why didn't one of the agents say something? Offer an idea? She looked behind her again. The first of the two SUVs was now close enough that she could see the two people in the front seat. She didn't recognize either of them. But then again, why would she? Ricky had so many people working for him that she could never totally keep track.

Her mouth felt like cotton but she forced her lips to work. "What now?" she whispered.

Neither agent spoke for a beat of a few seconds.

"We try to lose them," Jimmy finally offered. "There's got to be a turnoff coming up soon."

She sat back in her seat and pulled in a deep breath, held it and then expelled the air. She made herself repeat the exercise four more times, a trick her friend Abby, a paramedic, had taught her to fight panic. She closed her eyes and gave Calvin's fingers a squeeze. Prayer. That was what she needed now.

Father, please give Jimmy and Ryan wisdom and strength to help us all survive this ordeal. Please give me courage. Please keep Calvin safe.

Jimmy's sudden intake of breath stopped her thoughts and her eyes flew open. "What? What is it?" she asked. But she saw it before he could respond. The SUVs were gaining ground and gaining it rapidly. Already the front vehicle was practically beside them, with the second one closing in fast. Two seconds later, the van was trapped between them.

Her pulse, which had been racing ever since the sound of the first gunshot back at the house, seemed to accelerate even more. She held her breath as the van's wheels skidded along the pebbled shoulder before regaining traction. What was Jimmy doing? Had he lost control of the van on top of everything else? Behind her, she could hear Ryan muttering. She braced herself, one arm on the door handle and her body covering Calvin, and prepared for impact.

Bang. Bang. Bang.

The sound of gunfire echoed through the air. Half a second later, she once again felt the smooth surface of the blacktop beneath their wheels. She hadn't realized that she'd closed her eyes until she peeked them open again. What just happened?

"Nice shot!" Ryan offered from the back seat.

She snuck a glance out the side window. The black SUV that had been pressing against the passenger side of the van was gone. She turned around. The second vehicle was still behind them, but the first one had pulled along the side of the road and was growing smaller and smaller in the rear window.

"Did you shoot them?" she whispered.

"Nah. I couldn't get a clear shot. But I was able to hit at least one of the tires."

"Outrunning them isn't going to work." Ryan spoke up again, his voice less accusatory than before. "This van is no match against that Suburban. One jolt from behind and we'll go flying."

Jimmy didn't answer. Although maybe he couldn't hear the other agent's shouts over Calvin's wails. The panic she had been fighting since the first shots were fired had begun to rise like a tidal wave, ready to engulf her senses.

"Watch out!" Ryan yelled again. "They're right behind us."

Thud! Crunch!

The shuddering impact shouldn't have been startling. But somehow the reality of the popping air bags and acrid smell of burning wire jarred her out of panic as their vehicle listed sideways before coming to a stop. Dazed and shaken, she peered out the window, surprised to see that the collision had been worse for the SUV. A lone driver was slumped over the wheel as plumes of smoke engulfed the hood.

"Isobel!" Jimmy's voice was muffled but his message was clear. "Go! Grab the diaper bag and I'll get Calvin. Run."

Leave her baby? No way. Her hands were shaking as she pushed on the release button of the car seat. As if understanding the gravity of the situation, Calvin had ceased crying and was just staring up at her with his giant blue eyes.

"It's okay. Mama's here with you," she said as she wrenched open the side door of the vehicle. Without pausing to look back, she picked up her little boy and sprinted across the cornfield.

FOUR

The airbag had done what it was meant to do in cushioning the driver in the collision. But staying calm as he pushed aside the lifesaving balloon wasn't as easy as Jimmy would have expected.

He pulled in a deep breath as he considered the fate of the others. Isobel and the baby had apparently survived the crash with no major cuts or lacerations. And they were halfway across the field, closing in on the shelter of the trees. But Ryan hadn't fared nearly as well. By pulling on the steering wheel, Jimmy had hoped that the van would have completely avoided impact with the approaching SUV. But his attempt to outmaneuver their pursuers had been too little, too late. Instead of taking a direct hit from behind, the rear corner of the van had taken the brunt of the collision. The reckless turn may have lessened the injuries to Isobel and Calvin, but Ryan had been close to the point of impact.

Jimmy reached over the seat and did a quick assessment of his unconscious partner. Ryan's body was sprawled forward at an awkward angle and blood was trickling from the crown of his head. Jimmy pressed two fingers against Ryan's neck and heaved a sigh of relief. His partner's pulse was strong, which was a reason for hope, though it was impossible to determine the full extent of his injuries.

Jimmy pivoted his head again to check the damage on the other car. Also unconscious, the driver of the SUV remained behind the wheel of the vehicle, his airbag collapsed like a dying flower all around him. At least for the moment, he was one person who could be counted as out of the fray.

That left the two other combatants in the first SUV, which was still at least three hundred feet down the road where their tire had blown out.

There was no time to waste. Jimmy patted his pockets. He had two extra magazines that he'd taken when he'd grabbed the gun from Matt and five bullets in the chamber, but he was still outnumbered and outgunned. It would be better to head for the trees where he'd have cover to pick off their pursuers one on one. But that was a temporary solution at best. He remembered from studying maps of the area, if he was right about where they were, that there was a large lake not far from the road. He assumed that meant there would be houses. And sheds. And places where he and Isobel and Calvin could hole up until he came up with a better plan.

Whatever happened, it would definitely be useful to have another weapon.

He climbed out of the van and ran over to the wrecked SUV. His fingers were still shaking from the impact of the crash, but he kept his hand steady as he unclipped the driver's pistol from his shoulder holster and shoved it into the waistband of his pants. As he bent to snatch the extra magazines from the belt around the man's waist, a walkie-talkie on the passenger's seat buzzed with static. He pressed the talk button and an official voice crackled across the line.

"Pine Haven Police. Is that you, Ted?"

A wave of panic hit him hard as yet another avenue of escape seemed to close. With limited evidence, it was dangerous to jump to any definite conclusions, but the possibility of a connection between the police and Ricky's henchmen had to be considered. If even one member of the local law enforcement team was corrupt, it upped the stakes and made it even more vital that they proceed with caution.

As he sprinted back to the van, he turned to check the road behind them. Sure enough, the two men were headed in their direction, pistols drawn. He heaved out a sigh. They were still a considerable distance from Isobel, but they were closing in fast. He fixed his gaze on Ryan's still body in the back seat of the van as a cocktail of emotions swilled through his brain.

He couldn't leave him there. Partners didn't do that. But he needed to act fast. His fingers closed around the door handle and then, yanking as hard as he could, he wrenched the warped metal off its frame. With a hard tug, he dragged Ryan out of the van and propped his body against a stubby pine next to the road.

"Sorry to leave you here, friend," Jimmy muttered. Shaking off the pang of guilt pulsing in his chest, he took off after Isobel. For Ryan's sake, he hoped that it would be sooner rather than later that an alert passerby would call in the accident and an ambulance would arrive on the scene.

He caught up to Isobel seconds before she reached the trees. He took Calvin from her arms and turned for one final glimpse of what was happening behind them. Their pursuers had stopped at the site of the crash to check on their unconscious colleague, so he and Isobel would have a couple minutes' head start at least.

With Calvin snuggled against his shoulder, he matched Isobel's pace as they found themselves surrounded by a cathedral of pines. There was something eerily still about the landscape. But the unexpected tranquility after so much sensory overload gave Jimmy a strange feeling of disquiet. His panting breathes were too loud amid such a silence, and it took him a moment to realize that the surrounding hush meant they were still alone. At least for the moment. His chest was heaving from the exertion and sweat was rolling down his back as he turned to face Isobel. He could see that she was fighting back tears. "You still doing okay?"

She nodded, her smile wobbling.

"Hey," he said. "We're going to get out of this."

"No, Jimmy. You may honestly believe that, but Ricky always gets his way. No matter what I do, there is no way I can escape."

"Well, he didn't win this one. And he's not going to win in the end. And do you want to know why?"

Isobel lifted her head from her hands and looked at him, her eyes still huge with unshed tears. Jimmy felt his heart tighten with a protective surge.

"Because we're going to get you to the courthouse in Detroit in time for you to testify at the trial. And your ex-husband will be convicted and sent to jail. Okay?"

"I hope you're right, Jimmy. Let me take Calvin for a bit. I honestly think having him so close makes me run faster."

That was unlikely, but he wasn't going to argue.

"Why is it so quiet? Do you think the men who were chasing us have given up?"

"No. They're coming. That's for sure."

"So, what do we do then?"

"I'm working on it, but you'll be the first to know."

Isobel's body seemed to freeze. "Wait! Listen! I hear a siren. Do you think it's the police?"

Jimmy strained his ears. Isobel was right. Someone must have reported the accident and the cops had been called to the scene.

She reached over and touched his arm. "Shouldn't we go back and explain what happened?"

A prickle of dread threaded down his spine as he recalled the voice on the walkie-talkie.

"What?" she asked, reading his expression. "You don't think that's a good idea?"

Man, did he hate to be the be the one to wipe that look of relief off Isobel's face. But he didn't have any choice.

"The police can't help us now. We're on our own."

Isobel stared up at the weary face of Jimmy Flynn, waiting for him to crack a smile and laugh. Surely, he was joking. But, if anything, his jaw seemed to tighten and his eyes darken with a sort of resigned bleakness as he sighed and pushed a hand through his hair.

"I don't understand." The tears she had managed to stifle just moments ago again threatened to spill down her cheeks.

"We can talk about it later, okay? Let me take Calvin for a sec."

She set her son in Jimmy's arms as an icy current of dread snaked its way down her spine. Of course, she'd known that Ricky's influence extended beyond his crime family in Detroit, but she hadn't thought through what that actually meant. Her body shuddered as Ricky's face suddenly flashed before her eyes—his eyes black with hatred and a cruel smile twisting his thin lips.

"We can't even trust the police?" Her lips formed the words but the question was a whisper.

"We may have to, somewhere down the line. But for now, we proceed with caution. If Ryan…"

Her heart dropped in her chest. She had been so wrapped up in her own headspace that she hadn't thought about Ryan. Funny, kind, always the first to offer to help, he had initially been her favorite of the four agents assigned to her protective detail.

She took a trembling breath. "He's not—" She paused, unable to say the word.

"He was unconscious when I pulled him from the van. I hope that once the ambulance gets him to the hospital, he'll wake up with nothing more serious than a bad headache."

"I hope so, too, but…" Her words trailed off in surprise as they stepped out of the trees into what looked to be someone's backyard, complete with a trampoline and swing set. A wide driveway wound to the east, toward a small cabin visible through the trees. "Look," she said. "Maybe there is someone home who can help."

"No cars," Jimmy said, peering into the garage. "Just a power boat up on wheels." He walked toward the cabin and peeked into one of the windows. "The place looks closed up for the season. Probably owned by summer people who have packed up and gone home."

They walked to the back of the property for a closer look at the wide, clear lake that boasted of a number of smaller inlets. A spongy, weed-covered beach stretched for a few hundred yards to the north and then curved west along a rocky outcropping along the shore.

But directly in front of them was what could only be described as a breathtaking view. Sky-blue water shimmered in the clear October sun, the yellows and reds of the trees mirrored in the still water of the lake. Near the beach was a stone patio with a fire pit and three red Adirondack chairs facing north. Nearby, an Old Town canoe leaned against a shed, two paddles tucked underneath.

For the moment, it almost seemed as if they had stepped out of a nightmare into a beautiful dream. The sturdy cabin. The beautiful lake. The chairs around the fire pit, perfect for watching the sun rise. Maybe they could hide here indefinitely until the danger passed. But just that quickly, reality burst that bubble of hope. Ricky would never call his men back to Detroit while she was still alive, or at least, not until he had regained custody of Calvin.

Isobel felt her eyes fill with tears. She knew without a doubt that their pursuers would scour the area, going from house to house in search of their prey. Suddenly, the idyllic surroundings filled her with foreboding. With the lake on one side and the road on the other, they were effectively trapped and any hiding place they might choose was sure to be discovered sooner rather than later.

"How long do we have until they find us?" Isobel asked.

"Not sure. But we're not without resources. I have guns and ammo. And there's probably one cabin around here that has a phone."

"Who would we call?" The question died on her lips as Jimmy suddenly drew her in closer between him and Calvin.

Bang.

A bullet whizzed past her ear. Isobel pulled in a breath as a sudden suffocating mantle of fear seemed to squeeze her lungs closed.

"We're going be okay." Jimmy's breath felt warm against her ear. "We're not out of options. Can you paddle?"

"Paddle?" It took a moment for her to remember the canoe tucked against the shed.

As they dashed across the lawn, another spray of bullets exploded around them. Isobel gulped in another breath as Jimmy made easy work of pulling the canoe into the water. The boat swayed to the left and then the right as Isobel stumbled on board. Jimmy tossed the paddles and life jackets into the bottom, handed her the baby and then stepped into the lake, pushing the canoe farther in until the water was up to his waist. With a final thrust, he pulled himself on board as ice-cold waves flooded the bottom of the boat.

A moment later, the canoe was gliding forward as Jimmy dipped a paddle into the lake.

Isobel shivered as mud sloshed up and spattered against her legs. If she was cold, what must Jimmy be feeling? But at least they were safe.

Or were they? Isobel turned to scan the narrow strip of beach. The two men who had been so relentless in their pursuit continued to mark their progress as they walked along the shore.

Jimmy noticed them, too. "They're probably hoping to find another canoe or kayak so they can follow us."

"Do you think they will?"

He shook his head. "I doubt it. At least, not right away. And by the time they do, we'll be out of sight. We'll find a remote spot and make camp for the night."

Isobel nodded. It wasn't a long-term plan, but at least it would see them through to the next day. That seemed the best they could hope for at the moment.

Setting Calvin down in her lap, she picked up the second oar and began to paddle in tandem with Jimmy.

FIVE

She was wet and weary and exhausted to the bone when they reached a beach on a crescent-shaped inlet of the lake. No one seemed to have followed them, and to make sure no one would, Jimmy stowed the canoe safely out of sight.

Isobel kept pace with Jimmy as they forged a path through the tall, dry grass. Maybe the excitement of the last few days had jolted her senses into full alert, but between the fading colors of the surrounding trees and the ducks and geese tracing straight lines through the air, she couldn't remember ever seeing anything so beautiful.

"I was a city girl until I left Ricky and moved to North Dakota," she said, raising her eyes to look at Jimmy, who had Calvin cradled in his arms. She had to say that the little guy seemed to have taken a shine to the marshal. "But I've learned a lot about small town life." She paused and pointed to a tall wooden structure that looked like an oversize lifeguard chair nestled in a stand of thick trees. "What would you think about that deer blind as a place to spend the night?"

Jimmy looked skeptical. "It doesn't look all that comfortable. And what are the chances that the owner or owners are nearby?"

Isobel shrugged. "That wouldn't be the worst thing. But

it's hard to say who would hunting this week. Every state has a different season for deer, moose, coyote, muskrat..."

He grinned. "How do you know this stuff? And did you say moose?"

Before she could answer, Calvin began to wail.

"I'm going to need to nurse him since I don't have another bottle," she said. "Why don't I climb up and see what kind of shape it's in? Then we can decide whether or not to stay here or move on."

It was a good decision. The deer blind wasn't bad, all things considered. And it was a lot bigger than it looked from the ground. A lot more accommodating as well. An old braided rug covered most of the rough wood floor and two weather-beaten folding chairs were propped against the back of the structure. She opened one, dusted off the dirt from the seat and pulled it next to a large opening in the front that served as a window for hunters keeping watch on the forest floor.

"Looks perfect," she called down to Jimmy, who was halfway up the ladder with Calvin and the backpack of supplies.

"Take this," he said, handing her his jacket once her little boy was settled in her arms. "Use it to keep him warm."

"What about you? You must be freezing." Isobel shivered at the memory of the cold wet puddle sloshing at their feet on the bottom of the canoe. But not once had Jimmy mentioned his sodden boots and soaking-wet jeans. "We could look for matches and start a fire in that open space between the trees."

"Best not to call attention to our location," he said. "I'll dry off as I scout around and see if I can find a nearby town."

As Calvin closed his eyes and began to nurse, she drew

in a deep breath and basked in the familiar sense of joy of holding her baby close in her arms. But other emotions crowded her brain as well. Fear, of course, and uncertainty about what lay ahead. Gratitude toward God and toward Jimmy, who had made all the right moves in keeping them safe. A lump formed in her throat as she realized that at that very moment, Ryan could be fighting for his life in some small-town hospital.

The crackle of branches sent her senses into high alert. Jimmy? No. He wouldn't be returning this soon. An animal then, but definitely bigger than a squirrel. Whatever it was, it was on the move. The slim trunk of the aspen beside the blind quivered under its sparse canopy. Then, all at once, the shaking stopped and everything was still.

Isobel tore her glance away from the now-sleeping child in her arms toward the dappled shadows of autumn foliage. Something was out there; she knew that for sure. But it remained well camouflaged on the edge of darkness.

A soft padding sound drew her gaze to a dark shape clinging to the limb of a nearby pine. It moved its head slightly, giving her a sideways view of the speckled fur of a tawny bobcat. Its mustard-colored eyes with their dark black pupils met and held her stare.

Think! What did she know about bobcats? Not much, aside from the fact that, though small, they were capable of stalking much larger prey. Hard to believe since the animal poised on the branch wasn't much bigger than a well-fed housecat. And its soft pink nose and kitten-like purr made it seem more like a pet than a deadly predator.

And though the blind itself was open at the sides, it did offer some protection. On her own, she'd be confident in her ability to chase it away. But with a baby in her arms, she knew she was at a disadvantage. And bobcats were hunters, carnivores capable of climbing and pouncing in pursuit of a meal.

She calculated the distance between the tree and the deer blind. Ten feet? Maybe fifteen? Definitely too close for comfort. It wouldn't take more than a few seconds for this particular predator to reach the blind's protruding ledge. And then what? She searched the floor for something she could use to scare off the unwanted intruder. The folding chair? Too cumbersome. The diaper bag? Too soft and light.

She forced herself to look again into those glowing, marble-like eyes that had fixed on her visage with laser-like precision. Her heart pounded as she tightened her hold on Calvin.

"Isobel? Hey."

Relief washed through her senses at the sight of Jimmy staring up at her from the base of the blind. She felt the warmth of his intense gaze. And just like that, she wasn't afraid. Unlike Ricky, Jimmy would not turn his back when the going got tough. He seemed to care deeply about the safety and comfort of both her and Calvin, even beyond what the duties that were part of his job.

She shook off her sentimental musings and pointed toward the tree where the bobcat sat waiting. "We have a visitor."

"Okay. I see him." He bent down slowly and picked a branch off the ground. With one hand on his holster, he tossed it toward the tree.

Thwack! It hit the bark three inches below the bobcat's perch. The animal reacted with lightning speed, springing to a higher perch before disappearing into the trees.

A moment later, Jimmy was standing on the top rung of the ladder. "Okay if I join you?"

She smiled. "Of course. And thanks. You probably think it was silly of me to be scared of such a little cat but..."

"They can be fierce. How's the kid doing?"

"Good. It took a while but he finally fell asleep."

Jimmy opened the plastic chest, which had been set next to the back wall of the blind, and held up two blankets he found inside. "They look like they've been here for a while, but they'll go a long way in keeping all of us warm tonight. This one's not so bad," he said, draping a faded blue quilt across her shoulders and handing her the smaller one for Calvin.

"We already have your jacket. You keep the big one so you'll stay warm."

"I'll be fine." Jimmy unfolded a second chair and set it down in front of the opening. "I'll keep watch for a while just in case our friend comes back. And, hey. I almost forgot the good news. There's a town a short distance east of here. It looks small, but it probably has a bank or a store with an ATM where we can get money to buy a vehicle."

"So, we're definitely driving to Michigan?"

He nodded. "I figure that the guys who are after us have staked out the airports and bus stations. Besides, we'd need to show ID to get through security, which means that our names and itinerary could come under scrutiny. It would be best to stay off the radar for as long as we can."

Try as he might, Jimmy couldn't get comfortable on the rough wood floor. Isobel didn't seem to get much sleep either, curled up in the corner with an arm around Calvin. Come morning, it seemed that the little guy had been the only one to actually catch some real shut-eye.

But Jimmy must have slept for a least a couple of hours because when he woke up, there were patches of golden light breaking through the branches. He stood up and stretched and then, leaning against the open side of the blind, watched the sun rise through the shadows. The early sliver of morning felt like a thing of beauty that was his alone. He pulled in a lungful of clean, fresh air and checked his watch. Six a.m.

A few minutes later, Isobel joined him at the wooden rail.

"Breakfast?" she said as she pulled a protein bar from her backpack.

"Thanks. You have it. I'm not hungry." That wasn't true, but she didn't need to know that. She continued to rifle through the contents of the backpack, pulling out a diaper and a packet of wipes from somewhere inside.

"When Calvin wakes up, he's going to complain until he gets changed."

Ah, yes. He did know a little bit about babies. Not much, but enough to be coerced into change a diaper or two during the time at the safe house. The kid was cute, he'd give him that. And Isobel was a sweet and attentive mother.

Watching her care for her little boy, he couldn't help but think about the strange trajectory his own life had taken in recent years. If things had gone differently, he might have a child or two of his own by now. But it had probably all turned out for the best, as his middle sister loved to say. She'd made that claim so many times that he had almost started to believe it.

Almost, but not quite.

Reaching again into her backpack, Isobel pulled out a small bottle of water. She offered it to him now and he accepted it gratefully.

She waited until he had taken a long swig before restarting an old conversation. "Would you mind giving me a quick rundown of our plan for getting to Detroit?"

"Sure. We'll pack up this morning and head for town.

Best-case scenario, we find an ATM somewhere along the main street. I seem to recall that the maximum withdrawal is a thousand dollars, which won't be much, considering everything we need."

"I can take money out, too," she offered.

"That would help. But most machines are equipped with cameras, so our transactions will be monitored. I am hoping we'll be long gone before anyone picks up our trail." Of course, that was best case scenario. The faster they got off the grid the better. The agency would, no doubt, be tracking any digital activity, and, with the possibility of a mole, even this quick transaction could give away their location. Not that he was going to share these worries with Isobel. Best to stay positive. "We can use the cash to buy a used vehicle and maybe some food for the trip."

As plans went, it was pretty loose. But he felt hopeful as they headed into town, Calvin snug in a sling fashioned from his sweatshirt. It wasn't fancy, but it did the trick.

"One more thing," Jimmy said after they had been walking for a while. "I know you'd like to keep Calvin with you during the trial. But I was hoping you might reconsider."

She turned toward him and blinked. "You want me to leave Calvin. With whom?"

"I was thinking we could drop him off with a friend of my sister's who lives in Madison. She has five kids, so she knows a lot about babies."

Isobel shook her head. "I don't think so, Jimmy. I don't think he'd like that at all."

Jimmy shrugged. Of course, Calvin wouldn't like it. The kid had been the sole focus of his mother's attention for his entire life, so he'd certainly protest being left in the care of a person he had just met. But it was the best way to keep him safe—and to protect Isobel as well.

"I know you feel strongly about this. But Alice wouldn't let anything happen to him. And her kids would provide a good distraction."

Isobel pursed her lips and appeared to consider his suggestion. "Can I think about it? I won't say no, but I'm having trouble getting on board with the possibility."

"Fair enough," he said. He pointed to a clearing up ahead. "Look. The trail has widened, which means we're close to civilization."

Midmorning in Redling, Minnesota, life seemed to be moving at an easy pace. A few people were out strolling along the shallow stream that bisected the small three-block downtown. Young women pushing baby carriages, groups of older men moving along at a careful pace. Halfway down the main street was a small grocery store with an ATM in the lobby. They headed inside.

"I'll try to withdraw two thousand dollars and see what happens," Jimmy said as he punched a five-number code into the key pad. A digital message flashed—"Limit of one thousand dollars"—as twenty-dollar bills began to slide from the slot.

Jimmy pocketed the cash and then stepped aside for Isobel. It hadn't occurred to him until that moment that she might not have the money to cover the withdrawal to her account. But he didn't need to worry. Her success equaled his and her thousand-dollar contribution was added to the stash. Handing Isobel a couple of twenties for supplies, he planned his next move.

He had spotted an old Camaro with a sale sign parked in the lot next to the store, and he tracked down the owner in aisle five stocking shelves. The vehicle definitely was for sale. But the asking price was a couple thousand dollars more than they could afford.

Ater a bit of creative bargaining, a deal was struck. Eighteen hundred dollars to rent the Camaro for a week, with his grandfather's Rolex watch included as collateral. Thankfully, the man was looking to sell the car seat in the vehicle as well.

Seconds later, Isobel arrived at the front of the store, her voice pitched with excitement. "I got everything we needed—diapers, bottled water, a couple of sandwiches and some snacks."

He forced a smile. He had been hoping for something a bit more substantial. "Did you get any cookies or...?"

His words trailed off as a man in a tan jacket ambled through the sliding door. Jimmy stepped behind an end cap and motioned for Isobel to do the same.

"What's wrong?" she asked.

"Nothing we can't handle." He grabbed both bags and trained his glance on the clerk at the end of the aisle. "But right now, we need to get out of here fast. One of the shooters from the SUV just walked into the store."

SIX

Jimmy fixed his eyes on the road ahead, determined to stay focused on the positive. He didn't feel great about the fact that they had spent the last fifteen minutes ducking between parked cars in the Cenex lot, with a baby and two bags of groceries as they frantically tried to escape detection. Success at this point would be an open road with no one following them. Still, they had a long way to go before they reached Detroit. Good thing Isobel was such a trooper. She had buckled Calvin in the car seat and then taken charge of the food, opening a box of crackers and balancing it on the consol between the seats and then unwrapping a sandwich for him and setting it and a bottle of water next to him within easy reach.

He watched out of the corner of his eye as Isobel closed her eyes and said grace before digging into her lunch, grateful she didn't ask him to join her.

"How do you think they found us?" she asked after a bit.

He had been wondering the same thing. "They probably saw what direction we were headed on the lake and then zeroed in on the nearest town. But from here on out, we won't be quite so predictable."

"So, that's the plan then? Continue driving east and hope they don't figure out which route we're taking to Michigan."

He nodded. "That's pretty much it."

"Maybe we should consider finding a place to hide out and await backup from headquarters. All of this rushing around may not be necessary. The trial could be postponed, considering what happened to Stephanie."

"You could be right about that. But until we learn otherwise, we proceed on the assumption that you'll still be expected to take the stand."

"But I'm not the only witness." Isobel blew out a long sigh. "I'm not even an important one. Stephanie told me that since I wasn't privy to any specific details of Ricky's crimes, they'll only use my testimony to place him at the scene to back up other claims."

Jimmy nodded. He had heard that the feds had a decent case, even without Isobel's testimony.

"You nod, but are you even hearing me? I'm trying to stay calm here, Jimmy, but none of this makes any sense. No matter how you spin it, we have no backup in case of an emergency. If we knew who to trust, we could make a better plan."

"All true. But for now, we carry on the best we can."

"Sorry. I don't mean to put this whole thing on you. I'm sure you're just as confused as I am about why all of this went down. It's hard to believe that one of the team would deliberately sabotage their fellow agents and friends. Maybe it was just a slip of the tongue, something that got repeated to the wrong people. I could see that happening to someone like Stephanie, maybe. She's not a professional agent, so she could easily make a mistake."

"It's possible." He thought for a minute. "But not likely. She understands the implications of loose talk."

"Who then?"

He shrugged. That was the million-dollar question. Unlike Isobel, he didn't think the leak was an accident. Everyone involved in the protective detail was a pro, trained to avoid even the smallest mistakes. Ryan had been quick to point the finger at Len. But he hadn't explained why. Meredith? Maybe. But Jimmy couldn't see it. She didn't seem like the type to give up her friends in such a ruthless way.

"And why now?" Isobel couldn't seem to redirect her line of inquiry. "I was living at the safe house for almost six weeks. And all that time, no one bothered us at all."

"Maybe Ricky saw a chance and decided to take it."

"But how was he so sure that he'd succeed?"

"What do you think? You know him better than I do."

Zing. His response hit the mark. Isobel's eyes flashed as she turned to face him. "That's not true. Our entire marriage was based on a lie. Ricky was a master of artifice and deception."

Jimmy quickly backpedaled. "I didn't mean…"

"I know what you meant, Jimmy Flynn. You're thinking I have a direct pipeline into Ricky's brain. That I stayed with him as long as I did because it suited my purposes."

He shook his head. "I assure you I was thinking no such thing. In fact, I had just been marveling at how stoic you've been in facing so many challenges."

Isobel responded by closing her eyes and turning her head toward the window. Clearly, she was done with talking and wanted to sleep. So, that was it then. He missed the chance to assure her that if his words were sharp, it was unintentional, and that, like her, he was exhausted and in need of sleep.

In the back seat, Calvin appeared to be grabbing a bit of shut-eye, which seemed to be his specialty. The little boy's mouth was set in a grimace, his brow furrowed as if to show his dissatisfaction with the current state of affairs.

It was hard to blame him. The previous night in the deer blind had been brutal. Between the primitive sleeping arrangements, the cold and damp, and the fear that their hiding place would be discovered by the gunmen, it was little wonder that he and Isobel were running on empty.

Jimmy grabbed a handful of whole-wheat crackers that Isobel had left in the console between the seats.

A clear mind. That was what he needed as he considered what to do next. Just like Isobel, he had questions that begged for answers and an avalanche of doubts cascading through his brain. How many men were searching for them anyway? Given the long reach of Ricky's criminal organization, would it even be possible for them to stay off the radar all the way to Detroit? They were low on cash, which would mean a stop at another ATM, leaving yet another trail that pointed to their location. It was hard to accept, given all the issues with trust, but at some point, he might be forced to reconsider reaching out to the authorities.

Wrappings crinkled as he dug for the last few crackers, causing Isobel to open her eyes and stretch her arms toward the Camaro's low ceiling.

"Wow. That little catnap did me a world of good. Sorry about all of that stuff I said before. I tend to be hypersensitive about my marriage to Ricky."

"And I apologize for sounding so tetchy."

"You know so much about me. Why don't we talk about you for a change? Tell me something about your background."

Jimmy raised a brow. "What do you want to know?"

"Anything you want to share."

He thought for a moment. "I grew up in Portland. Big, extended family, lots of uncles and aunts. I'm the oldest of four kids. My younger sisters are great, but they have a lot of ideas about what kind of car I should drive, where I should live and who I should be friends with... But despite my need for constant guidance, I'm still their first call when any appliance breaks or malfunctions."

"I wondered at your being so good at plumbing."

"What?" He was confused until he remembered that back at the safe house he had always been the one to tighten the faucets or unclog the drains. "Yeah. Plumbing skills are my superpower."

"You do seem kind of domestic."

He grinned. "I'm not sure you mean that as a compliment."

"I do. You have a competent, helpful vibe going for you, so much so that I assumed you were a family man with a wife and kids. And, of course, there's the fact that you own a minivan."

Jimmy laughed. "Say what you want, but it fits a lot of stuff, especially when the seats are out. And to answer your question, no, I've never been married. I did come close once, but that's a story for another day."

"Well, if you change your mind, I'm here to listen," Isobel offered. "We're stuck here in the car with plenty of time for conversation."

He pulled in a deep intake of breath. He really didn't like to talk about Kim, his ex-fiancée, and what had happened on the eve of their wedding. But there was something about Isobel that made him want to open up and say more. But, as usual, he took refuge in silence.

Besides Isobel seemed determined to keep the conversation personal. "So, you're not married and you're far away from your family and you work out of Detroit. Do you have a girlfriend?"

He shook his head. "Not at the moment."

"I find that surprising…"

A wave of warmth surged through his chest, and he was surprised that such an offhanded comment could fill him with such pleasure. "I've been pretty focused on work."

"Makes sense. Judging from what has happened so far in this case, it's clearly an intense job. So, Marshal Flynn." She turned to face him with a wide grin. "How many witnesses have you protected so far in your career?"

He quirked a smile. "How old do you think I am?"

"Not old at all. I was just curious about how long you've worked at this particular job."

"Only a couple of years. This is a second career for me."

"What was your first career?"

"I was a therapist."

"Oh, wow." Isobel's face registered surprise. "I would never have guessed. You seem so—" She struggled to find the right word. "Not exactly easygoing, but definitely willing to accept people the way they are, without analyzing their every move."

"I'm intrigued why you think that about me."

"Well. I suppose I was remembering the drive to the safe house. Ryan was the one asking all the questions about Ricky and wanting to hear all the details of how we met. He said that I didn't seem like the type to go for an older, rich guy. I didn't mind it coming from him, but stuff like that really bothers me. The point is that you didn't say anything, and I appreciated that. Because I really am a lot different now than I was when I married Ricky."

"Of course you are. People change. They get older and wiser."

"True. But throughout my life, people have always tried to put me in boxes. Acting like they've figured me out since I'm not very complicated."

"You want to be complicated?" Jimmy raised a brow.

"Maybe not complicated. Just unique. Doesn't everyone want that?"

"I guess. But full disclosure here. I read your file, so I know your father is a child psychologist."

"Is that why they assigned you to my case?"

"Maybe. But you can be assured that the only box I aim to put anyone in is a jail cell. And that will be your ex-husband, Ricky."

"Ha," she said. "I'm glad I don't have to worry about you psychoanalyzing my behavior. Between my dad and Ricky, I've probably had enough of that to last a lifetime."

Now it was his turn to laugh. "I don't do that to my friends."

After a few moments of silence, Isobel spoke again. "Okay, friend. Just so you know, I can take over driving anytime if you need a break."

"Thanks. I'm okay for now."

"Well, you don't need to come across as a superhero just to prove a point. See? I'm pretty good at ascribing motives if given a chance, even when it comes to marshals who saved my life. So, if you won't let me take a turn behind the wheel, at least let's stop and get some real sleep soon. I think we're both exhausted."

As they crossed the St. Croix River to Wisconsin, Isobel spotted a sign for a chain motel a mile off the highway in Hudson.

"That might be a good place for us to stay," she said. "And cheers to one state down with a couple more to go."

"You seem chipper at the thought of sleeping in a real bed. Maybe this would be a good time for us to talk about leaving Calvin with my friend Alice."

Isobel pulled a face. "I'm thinking no."

"Why?"

"Well, first of all, I don't know anything about this person. And second, I thought you said she was your sister's friend. Now you're calling her your friend. Which is it, anyway?"

"Can't it be both? Alice was my middle sister's roommate in college, and she spent a lot of time with my family."

"And…" Isobel prompted.

"There is no 'and.' That's all there is to it. The two of them stayed in contact after graduation. You need to understand that my sister is the kind of person who can't resist sharing even the most inconsequential details about people she knows. So, over the years, I've heard a lot about what's going on with Alice and her family. And there are a few other good reasons why she'd be a good choice to care for Calvin. I haven't seen or been in contact with her for years, so there's no chance she'll be on anyone's radar. Second, and also key, her place is right off the highway in Madison. And, most of all, you'll like her. I guarantee it. She actually reminds me a lot of you. She's kind and has an optimistic spirit, even though she's been through some hard times and nothing in her life has been all that easy."

Isobel tucked back a smile, unwilling to show that she was flattered by the comparison. "What do you think she'd say if her college roommate's brother shows up out of the blue and asks her to watch some random kid?"

"She'll say yes."

"Because she's so nice."

"No. Because when I explain the situation, she'll agree that it's important to keep Calvin safe."

"But what about her? How can we be certain that Alice

and her family will be safe? What if Ricky somehow figures out the connection?"

"That's not going to happen. Besides, Alice's husband, Patrick, is a former Marine. I assume their house has state-of-the-art security system to protect them from intruders."

"Right turn here." Isobel pointed to the sign for the Best Western at the next exit. "Can I ask one more thing?"

Jimmy nodded.

"Why is it so important that I leave Calvin behind anyway? You know what happened when he was born. How Ricky tried to kidnap him and how I spent eight hours in the hospital thinking I may have lost him forever."

"I know all of that, but..."

"No. Let me finish. The moment I finally knew he was okay, I made a vow to be there for him, no matter what. So, how can I be sure he'll be safe with a person I've never met when the only thing I know about her is that she's a friend of the man I hardly know?"

"A man you hardly know?" Jimmy raised a brow. "Wow. How quickly I've been demoted."

His eyes were alight, and she knew he was teasing. Still, it was a side of Jimmy she hadn't seen before and she liked it. She was curious to learn more about him and found herself wishing they could be real friends apart from their current situation. Her heart warmed at the thought. But that wasn't their reality. The fact was that she and Calvin were in danger because she'd put her trust in the wrong man. She wouldn't let her guard down so easily again.

Jimmy's expression softened. "I understand your concerns. And I know what Ricky is capable of. But that's the very reason you should leave your son with Alice. Sure, the little guy will miss you. But he'd have lots of big kids around to distract him. And having a nine-month-old baby along for the drive makes my job that much harder."

As Jimmy pulled the Camaro under the covered entryway of the hotel, Isobel turned her face to the window to hide the unexpected tears that had filled her eyes. It was hard to discount the logic of what Jimmy had said. But she wasn't ready to leave her son with his friend in Madison, no matter how nice she supposedly was.

Outside, it was almost dusk, but the landscaping lights around the motel were warm and welcoming. Jimmy stepped out of the car, leaning inside before he closed the door.

"I'll try to pay with cash, so the charge can't be traced. And if it's not too expensive, I'll get us a suite."

"Don't forget to ask for a porta-crib," she said, swiveling around to face Jimmy.

If he noticed her red eyes and tear-stained face, he didn't mention it. "I won't forget," he said, opening his wallet and counting out four fifty-dollar bills. "Tomorrow, we can stop and get more money for the rest of the trip. Back in a flash," he said as he closed the Camaro's door.

She waited until he disappeared inside the lobby before climbing into the back seat.

"How are you doing back here, little guy?" she said as Calvin stared at her with worried eyes. She reached over to stroke his cheek. "I know this hasn't been easy for you, stuck in this seat for hours, without being able to move around. I'm trying to figure out what's best for you, but turns out, that's not so simple. The thing is, Jimmy's pretty smart and he thinks it would be a good idea for you to spend a few days without me. Apparently, his friend Alice has kids who will make it so much fun that you might not even miss me at all."

Calvin treated her to a gummy smile.

"You want to think about it, right? I get it. So do I. It's a big step for us. But I'm starting to realize that we may need to trust Jimmy on this, okay?"

The car door opened and Jimmy slid back inside. "All good. Got the suite and the porta-crib. I'll pull in closer to the building."

Once the car was parked, Isobel lifted Calvin out of his seat and followed Jimmy through the lobby.

Bing! As the elevator jolted to a stop on the fourth floor, Calvin's cries of complaint turned louder, reaching a fever pitch as they moved down the hall to their suite. Jimmy opened the door with the key card and headed straight for the bedroom closet where the porta-crib was stored. With a turn of the wrist, he shook it open and pushed the thin mattress in place.

"Take your time settling the baby," Jimmy said, backing slowly out of the room. "I'll wait out here. Give a shout if you need anything."

"Sure." Isobel nodded, though she couldn't imagine what that would be. She poured herself a glass of water from the sink and, with Calvin in her arms, she sat down in the armchair next to the bed and began to nurse. After the awkwardness and discomfort of caring for him in the blind and at rest stops, this was so much more relaxing,

Until it was time to ease him into bed. Real tears filled his eyes and his lips trembled with anxiety. It took a moment for her to understand that he was missing Bingo, the stuffed bear he liked to cuddle at bedtime in his crib.

She checked, but it wasn't with the any of the gear they had carried to the room. Setting Calvin down in the porta-crib, she did another quick search through the backpack, but she failed to come up with the missing stuffie.

Think, Isobel. Think.

Then—a flash of inspiration. The stuffed bear had definitely been wedged next to Calvin's car seat when Jimmy had gone into the motel to book the room. She recalled making a mental note not to forget it. Then, out of sight, out of mind—it must have been dropped or forgotten in the lobby in the rush and confusion.

The solution was to ask Jimmy to go downstairs to look for the missing stuffie. Hadn't he said that she should call him if she needed anything?

She walked across the bedroom and opened the inner door of the suite.

"Jimmy?" she said softly.

No answer.

"Jimmy?" she tried again.

He was sound asleep.

She could try shaking him awake and asking him to retrieve the bear, but wouldn't it be easier to just do it herself? It wouldn't take long. Five minutes tops, probably less.

She checked on Calvin. He was also asleep.

Even so. He was sure to wake up and want his stuffie. Better to do this now than in the middle of the night.

She slipped the key card into the pocket of her jeans and tiptoed out the door.

SEVEN

As the elevator lurched downward, second thoughts began to crowd Isobel's head. Maybe she should have woken Jimmy and asked him to retrieve Bingo. But did he even know what the little bear looked like? And all she needed to do was retrace her steps through the lobby and into the parking lot.

She stiffened her resolve. This was for the best. Sure, Calvin had temporarily settled down without his bedtime buddy, but it would only be a matter of time before he woke up missing Bingo.

She drummed her fingers on the handrail of the elevator. The conversation in the car had been interesting, to say the least. When she had asked Jimmy if he was married, he had answered forthrightly, admitting he had gotten close to walking down the aisle without providing any details. There was something about the agent that warned against personal questions. And yet, without much prodding, he had admitted to once working as a shrink.

A shrink. Ugh. A shiver of dismay crept up her spine.

Psychology was not her thing. It had been a constant source of frustration to the only child of a psychiatrist father who reveled in placing himself in the role of judge and jury, always eager to predict and explain her moods and actions and offer advice accordingly. Like when she'd let her grades slip. Or dropped out of her high school production of *The Music Man*. He'd just nod and remark with a sage smile that of course she needed to find a way of rebelling. It was all in keeping with her character. He had claimed to know her better than she knew herself. And worst of all, he had smirked knowingly when she married Ricky. Like he knew she would be bowled over by superficial niceties. Like it was exactly what he would have expected from someone with low self-esteem.

She sighed. She wasn't being fair. Her mom and dad had been good parents. They had showed up at her track meets and helped her figure out her geometry proofs. Actually, they were probably more involved in her life than she'd ever manage to be with Calvin. Being a single parent was hard, and it was just going to get harder. That's why she was so grateful for the community she had in Dagger Lake. Having a bank teller for a mom meant that Calvin wasn't going to enjoy all the finer things he might have experienced if she had stayed married to Ricky—trips to Europe, private tennis lessons, a home chef. But money couldn't buy happiness, as she knew all too well.

The elevator jerked to a halt on the ground floor. Isobel sighed again, grateful to have her musings cut short. She hated to consider what Calvin was going to miss because of her reduced circumstances.

She stepped off the elevator and allowed her eyes to do a sweep of the hallway floor. No dropped stuffie. It was only about fifteen feet to turn the corner to the main lobby, but again, no sign of Bingo. There was still the possibility that he had been dropped in the parking lot. Or maybe someone had picked him up and turned him into the lost and found.

She strode over to the front desk and rang the bell. Five

second later, a disheveled twentysomething woman wearing a pin that read Night Manager popped out from a back room.

"Sorry. I was just gathering used towels from the pool. We're understaffed, so I'm working solo. How can I help you?"

"I checked in just a little while ago, but I seem to have lost my son's stuffed animal. It's a teddy bear. I was wondering if anyone turned it in."

"Yes! Another guest found it in the entryway. I've got it right here." The woman reached under the counter and pulled out Bingo.

Isobel released an audible sigh as relief bloomed across her chest. "Thank you so much. My little guy is going to be mighty grateful about this."

"Glad I could help. I suppose I better see about getting those towels into the wash. Let me tell you, these industrial-style machines are something else." She turned away and disappeared into the back.

Isobel looked at Bingo for another moment. Light brown and already ragged from all the love, the little bear had only been in Calvin's possession for a few weeks but he already seemed like a member of the family. Perhaps her little boy had become too attached to his favorite stuffie. But then again, she'd read in more than one of her parenting books that kids craved stability and routine. Given all that Calvin had endured in his nine short months of life, he'd more than earned a little attachment to his favorite stuffed animal.

As she tucked Bingo under her arm, her senses went into high alert, activated by the swish of the entryway doors opening and the sight of two men entering the lobby.

Both were familiar from the shoot-out at the lake.

Warning bells sounded in her head. How had their pursuers found them here? That didn't matter now. Should she shout for help? But the manager was in the back, working on the laundry. Would she even be able to hear sounds of distress? How to escape? That was the question that mattered. The only question that mattered.

All she was sure of was that she needed to get out of there fast.

She took off in a full-out sprint, desperate to put as much distance as she could between her and her assailants. She knew they were behind her. She could hear the thudding of feet against the laminate floor. Her heart pounded as her brain crystalized a new concern—Calvin. She couldn't return to their room. That would be like leading the wolves to a lamb. Maybe, if she could get outside the hotel, she could find a place to hide.

She dashed past the elevator she had taken to the lobby. Up ahead was a doorway at the end of the hall. With a few quick strides, she was there, turning the knob, ready to lead them somewhere, anywhere, away from Calvin. But the door didn't open to the outside. Instead, there was just a dimly lit stairwell leading in only one direction—up.

She gripped both sides of the railing and took the stairs two at a time. She'd just made it to the first landing when the door below her crashed open, followed by a hesitant tread beneath her on the stairs. She glanced down through the grated metal. Only one man was following her. Where was the other one? Did he know the room where Calvin was sleeping?

Terror coiled in her chest. She willed her legs to keep moving, but she could feel herself slowing down as weariness swamped her body, her limbs growing leaden with regret. Was it even worth her efforts to get away when it all seemed so futile? When Ricky's surrogates always found her? She'd fled to North Dakota. They'd found her. The safe house? They'd found her. Now, an off-the-grid hotel? Of course, they had tracked her there. Ricky was determined to gain custody of Calvin, and he always made good on his threats.

But no, she couldn't let him take his son. Her son. Her precious boy. What did it matter if Ricky's men had found them time and time again? Time and time again, God had provided and led them to safety. And even if the men located her room, Jimmy was there to protect Calvin. She couldn't lose faith now. Lowering her head, she renewed her resolve and charged ever upward. How many floors were in this motel? As she passed the third landing, it became clear that her pursuer was gaining on her.

Gasping in air, she pushed forward, her legs burning from the exertion as she turned to continue up the next flight. She'd already taken three steps when her mind registered what her eyes saw. This was the last stairwell.

She had reached the fourth floor. Where Calvin was sleeping.

Momentum carried her up two more steps before she turned around. The sudden change of direction was disorienting, but she reached out to steady herself against the railing. She caught herself and held still for the span of one heartbeat. And then she charged down the stairs.

But the man chasing her was much larger than she had realized.

And she was moving too fast.

Every part of her being felt out of control.

Only one thought remained constant—protecting Calvin. And that meant doing everything in her power to prevent this man from finding her son.

A half second later, she collided with her pursuer. Unprepared for a frontal assault, he stumbled backward, taking her with him as he fell down the stairs.

There was a sharp explosion of pain as her head hit the steps. And then nothing.

Jimmy's eyes blinked open, exhaustion causing a fleeting moment of disorientation as his eyes scanned the room. Where was he? A second later, he remembered that he had fallen asleep while Isobel settled Calvin. He rubbed a hand against his jaw, feeling the prickles of two days' worth of stubble as anxiety began to gnaw at his mind. It was quiet. Too quiet.

He glanced at the porta-crib. Nestled against the mesh side, Calvin was sound asleep, his chest rising and falling in regular intervals, accompanied by soft snores. Well, if Calvin was there, Isobel couldn't be far away. He knew by now that she was extremely protective of her son. Not that he could blame her, given everything she'd been through. Still, he didn't like the fact that she wasn't in either the bedroom or the bathroom.

He stood up, his hand automatically confirming that his pistol was still in its holster. With one more glance around the suite, he snagged his hotel key card and opened the door a crack. He peered up and down the hallway. No sign of Isobel. Could she have gone to get ice? Or returned to the car for something?

Apprehension tightened across his chest. He should have warned her to not leave the room. Strike that. He shouldn't have allowed himself to sleep so soundly that he wouldn't notice if she opened the door. That was Marshal Training 101. Should he try to track her down? But that would mean leaving Calvin on his own, and he didn't like the idea of that either.

Besides, there was no way Ricky and his men could have found them here. Well, not no way. There was never a zero percent chance of anything. But the odds were essentially negligible. And while Ricky's influence might have a long reach, it just wasn't in the realm of possibility that the Detroit mobster could have predicted they would stop at this particular hotel in this particular town. The statistics didn't account for it. No doubt, Isobel would return in just a few minutes with a perfectly good explanation of where she had been.

Jimmy frowned. Regardless of the facts, he was uncomfortable not knowing where she had gone. He turned back toward the hotel room. He didn't want to leave Calvin. But if Isobel didn't turn up in another minute, he'd have to go and find her.

Ping. The elevator at the end of the hallway signaled its arrival on their floor. Jimmy heaved a sigh and prepared to give Isobel a gentle but stern rebuke about wandering away on her own. She was his witness and he needed to know where she was at all times.

The elevator door slid open and the sigh of relief died on his lips. Not Isobel then. The man on the elevator was one of Ricky's henchmen. Jimmy quickly pulled his head back into the room but continued to watch through the crack in the door.

What? How? His brain scrambled to understand. It didn't make sense that they had been followed to this small motel a mile off the interstate. And if Ricky's man was here, where was Isobel? Had they already grabbed her and were coming for Calvin?

Without taking his eyes off the man, he reached for his pistol and prepared to engage. But the interloper didn't even glance down the hall. Instead, he looked at his phone and then turned and walked toward the stairwell. As soon as he was out of sight, Jimmy slipped out the door, pulling it closed behind him.

In less than ten seconds, he had reached the entryway to the stairwell. He pushed open the door and took in the details of the situation. The flickering light providing a dim glow. The sound of pounding footsteps along the metal stairs. The body of an unconscious man sprawled on the landing. And a visibly shaken Isobel, struggling to get to her feet.

Anger tightened across his chest as he raised the Glock to take aim. But in the confines of the stairwell, there was no room for error. If the bullet missed its mark, it would ricochet off the concrete walls and could end up hitting Isobel. And already, in his moment of hesitation, the man had almost reached her side. This was not the time for gunfire. Swallowing a few choice words, Jimmy shoved his pistol into his pants and then threw himself down the stairs.

The impact should have knocked the breath out of him, but he had wrapped his arms around his attacker's torso so tightly that they both rolled across the landing and down the next flight of stairs. He tucked his head to prevent injury, but Ricky's henchman didn't seem to be sustaining any damage either as he unpinned one of his arms and then proceeded to use it to pummel Jimmy's back as they thudded in tandem onto the landing.

Jimmy scrambled upright and risked a glance toward the top of the stairs. Relief bloomed in his chest. Isobel was now a full flight above them, but she still looked disoriented. She must have hit her head fighting her assailant.

"Run, Isobel!" he shouted. "Get Calvin and get out of here."

His words seemed to penetrate her malaise as she responded with a tight movement of her chin.

Whack! A sharp pain reverberated across his abdomen as a punch landed squarely against his left side, followed by the suffocating sensation of an arm being wrapped around his neck. He pulled his head back quickly, making contact with his assailant's nose. Moving fast, he pivoted to face his opponent. Distracted by the blood pouring out of his nose, the other man wasn't prepared as Jimmy landed three quick blows to his stomach.

But the guy wasn't about to go down without a fight. He lurched forward, even as Jimmy continued to throw punches, and, using his momentum, collapsed against Jimmy.

Jimmy fought against his natural instinct to crumple under the other man's frame. He kicked out his opponent's legs and then dropped into a somersault and rolled.

Thud. Without his own body to break the fall, the other man landed hard against the stairs. And there he remained, motionless.

Jimmy scrambled upright, his heart drumming in his chest, and surveyed the scene before him. Both of Ricky's men were knocked out on the stairs, each a flight apart. He pulled the Glock out of his pants and walked toward the man collapsed in front of him. Holding the pistol in hand, he whacked him on the head, hard. Then he climbed the stairs and did the same to the second assailant, making sure they remained unconscious for as long as possible.

Then he took a deep, steadying breath and ran a hand through his hair. Adrenaline coursed through his body as he realized that Isobel was no longer in the stairwell. He could only hope that she had packed up Calvin and left the hotel. A dull throbbing pain emanated down his temples as he rolled his head back on his neck. Would she wait for him? Or would she just drive away?

He could only hope that he would find her curled up in the passenger seat of the Camaro. Because one part of this evening's ambush remained niggling in his brain, like an itch he couldn't scratch, like a mystery begging to be solved. How had the men found them?

Taking the stairs two at a time, he quickly reached the ground floor. He opened the door leading to the lobby and, relieved to see that no one was manning the front desk, he continued on his way. In a few quick strides, he was jogging toward the Camaro. The engine was running and Isobel was sitting in driver's seat, waiting. She had done everything exactly right.

He opened the passenger door. "Let me take the wheel."

She shook her head. "I'm so amped up. I need to do something. I'd like to drive for just a little while to settle down."

"But your head. Weren't you knocked out?"

"Look, do you want to sit here arguing? Let's get out of here."

Jimmy paused only a second longer before swinging his body into the car. She was right. At any moment, another guest could find one of the men in the stairwell. And then the police would be called. The very best thing they could do was put as many miles between themselves and the hotel as quickly as possible.

The car was already moving as he pulled on the seat belt. He could see the signs of stress on Isobel's face. Her lips were clenched and her eyes looked strained. He waited until they were on the freeway before speaking up.

"I really am worried about your head. I know what the effects of an encounter like this one can do. You feel keyed up and ready to take on the world. But soon you are going to feel sapped of energy."

Isobel cast a glance in his direction. "I know. Just let me be in control for a little bit. That's all I want. A moment where I don't feel like my whole life is a roller coaster with someone else in charge."

Well, he could understand that. And, there was something he needed to do that might require a bit of concentration. Reaching around into the back seat, he snagged the diaper bag that had accompanied them from the safe house. One by one, he removed the items. When the bag was empty, he ran his hands along the seams. Nothing.

"Did you find what you were looking for?" Isobel asked as he replaced the items back into the bag.

"No." Frustration made his answer curt. "Why did you leave the room again?"

"Calvin dropped Bingo. But I didn't want to wake you up."

"Bingo?"

"You know, his stuffed bear?"

Bingo! Of course. He turned and gently lifted the stuffed animal out of Calvin's sleeping grasp. His ran his hand through the fur. There! A small incision along the seam. He pushed his fingers inside, smiling with satisfaction as they closed around a nickel-size piece of hardware.

No wonder Ricky's men had been one step ahead of them. They had been using a tracker to monitor their every move.

EIGHT

Midnight found Jimmy once again behind the wheel of the Camaro.

The sixty dollars left in his wallet was earmarked for gas, but that was the least of his concerns. He and Isobel were exhausted, and the idea of pulling into a rest stop and tucking in for the night seemed foolhardy given that outside temperatures had dipped down to the forties. A faded billboard offering cheap accommodations made the decision for him. Five minutes later, he was standing at check-in, counting out five tens and two one-dollar bills, the bargain rate for latecomers at the budget hotel.

"Does that include tax?" Jimmy asked, digging into his pocket for loose change.

"Whatever, man," the clerk said with a yawn.

It was probably not the time or place to ask about a porta-crib or the possibility of a complimentary breakfast. They could make a nest of blankets for Calvin on the floor and pick up some coffee when they stopped for gas in the morning.

Best of all was the certainty that no one would know they would be spending the night at the Riverview Inn, a mile off the exit in a small town in Wisconsin. A trace of a smile formed on Jimmy's lips as he thought about the rest stop in Hudson and the spare tire on the back of that west-bound RV where he had tucked the tracker.

Calvin buried his head against Jimmy's shoulder as they trudged through the lobby and down the hall to their room. He didn't even stir when Jimmy laid him on a quilt on the floor and tucked Bingo under his arm.

"He's down for the count." Jimmy regarded the little boy with a tender smile. "We should follow suit. Why don't I take the bed closest to the door?"

Isobel nodded. Leaning against the wall, she kicked off her shoes. There would be no talk tonight about future plans. After thirty-five hours on the run, what they needed was sleep.

For Jimmy, morning came far too early, heralded by shafts of sunlight streaming in from the sides of the room-darkening drapes. He pushed up on his elbow and looked at the clock by the bed. Seven thirty. Isobel and Calvin were still asleep, so he tiptoed across the room to use the facilities. His stomach growled, reminding him that it would be lunchtime when they arrived in Madison.

Isobel was sitting up in bed when he pushed open the bathroom door.

"I was having the most awful dream. It was about Ricky and he…" She trailed off, shaking her head. "It was frightening, but not in the usual way. I was drowning, and he was trying to help me. He said I was a good mother to our son."

Jimmy blew out a long breath. It was tempting to ask for more details, but he didn't want to sound like a therapist. Best to change the subject.

"That reminds me of something I wanted to ask you about Calvin's stuffed bear. Where did he get it?"

Isobel shook her head. "I found it on the changing table

I assumed it came from Ryan since he had been shopping in town. I intended to follow up with him but then I forgot."

Ryan…he thought once again about the man accusing Len. Was it to throw Jimmy off? But his partner had tried to help them escape and been seriously, maybe fatally, injured in the process. He felt a twinge of guilt at having left the young man behind and hoped he'd gotten help in time. "No worries. Even if you knew who gave Calvin the teddy bear, that wouldn't necessarily tell us who planted the tracker, or when and why." He sat down to tie his shoes, which he had discarded on the floor. "I was thinking about heading to the lobby to see if I can scare up a cup of coffee for breakfast."

"I'll wash up and keep an eye on Calvin." She shifted her glance to the little boy, whose eyes were still closed, his hands balled into two tight fists. "Wait," she said as he turned the handle on the door. She opened the flap of the backpack and pulled out a protein bar, which was smashed and misshapen. "Do you want this?"

Jimmy shook his head. "You have it. I'm still hoping this place will have some sort of buffet, even if it's only bagels and fruit. What can I get you if they do?"

"Orange juice," she said. "If it's on the menu."

He'd check, but he had low expectations.

The breakfast bar, however, turned out to offer a far better spread than he'd hoped for. Bananas. Apples. Even orange juice and those miniature boxes of cereal he'd loved as a kid. He piled everything up and then added a couple of spoons and cartons of milk to a cardboard carrier. Not a bad haul.

He wasn't in any rush to get back to the room. He poured a cup of coffee from a carafe on the counter and took a seat in the breakfast nook where a handful of other guests had commandeered the tables closest to the electric fire. It was hard to blame them. Even inside the hotel, there was a chill in the air.

It had been a good decision to stop here. They'd needed a good night's sleep and time to recover from their injuries, and the complimentary breakfast would save them money down the road. He tucked in a smile as he tore open a box of Cheerios and added some milk. Plus, it would have been cold and miserable to spend the night in the car, turning on the heater every half hour and watching the fuel gauge slowly dip toward empty. The downside was that they were now almost completely broke, with little money left for gas and other essentials. With that in mind, he headed back to the buffet and added a couple of bagels to his stash.

Returning to the table, he took a moment to think about the repercussions of what had happened the night before. No wonder it had been impossible to shake the men following them from the safe house. How had he failed to recognize that there was no logical way to explain their pursuers' ability to pinpoint their movements so accurately? At least they had been safe from detection the night they had spent in the wilderness.

But the fact remained that someone had embedded a tracker in Calvin's stuffed bear. And two days removed from the assault on the safe house, Jimmy was still no closer to discovering the identity of the mole. Or the reasons behind the betrayal. He considered reaching out to his supervisor, US Marshal Merle Miller, and explaining why he was currently off the grid and that he still had the witness in protective custody. But the possibility that his message might be intercepted by a corrupt member of the agency wasn't worth the risk.

Still, his original assignment remained the same—protect the witness. But there were so many uncertainties involved in that task. He had told Isobel that he expected the trial to proceed without Stephanie Marsh. But was that true? He needed to find out what was happening before they arrived at the courthouse.

He took his last sip of coffee and tossed his cup into the bin. No matter what, it seemed prudent to continue on course with the original plan.

When he got back to the room, Isobel was sitting on a chair watching as Calvin scooted across the floor. He handed her a carton of orange juice and set the cardboard tray with the rest of the breakfast items next to the TV on the counter.

"Do we need to leave right away?"

Jimmy shrugged. "Checkout isn't for another couple of hours."

"Good. I was thinking I might cut up a banana for Calvin. Also—" She paused as she gathered her son in her arms. "While you were gone, I was weighing the pros and cons of leaving him with your friend. And the truth is, I wouldn't be totally opposed to the idea. With one caveat. I'd like to meet her first and see how it goes."

Excellent. This was what he had been hoping she would say.

"But," she continued, "I'd still like to hear how you think it's going to go down when you show up unexpectedly on her doorstep with a woman and a baby."

"Ideally, I'd call her and explain. But I don't know her cell number, and the only way to get it would be to contact my sister. And I'd rather not take that chance."

"Because they might be tapping your sister's phone?"

"Yeah. And I'd prefer to stay off the radar for as long as we can." He looked at Isobel and shook his head. "I admit that this situation is not ideal. But we're almost out of cash, and at this point, our options are limited. Alice will definitely be surprised to see me, but she'll for sure want to help. If at any point you don't feel comfortable, we'll scrap the plan and take Calvin with us."

A carton of orange juice and a box of raisin crunch went a long way in lifting Isobel's spirits. Calvin must have been feeling some of that positive energy as well, because he was all smiles as she clipped him into his car seat, though he resisted all attempts to dislodge the sodden piece of her bagel grasped in his hand.

But Jimmy seemed distracted when they finally hit the road, his brow furrowed as he shifted in and out of the passing lane around convoys of the semis heading east.

"Um… Isobel? I'd like to suggest a change in our itinerary."

Uh-oh. Was Jimmy having second thoughts about stopping in Madison? That would be a problem since she was pretty much on board with the idea of leaving Calvin with his friend by now.

"Okay," she said hesitantly.

"We're on track to arrive at Alice's in the early afternoon. But what would you say to making a quick stop at a library?"

"Why?"

"Well, I was thinking about your question on whether the trial would go forward without Stephanie. I originally thought yes. But now I'm not so sure. There is a chance that the judge might have agreed to a continuance."

"But how would it change things? Don't we still need to check in with the marshals and fill them in about what happened at the safe house?"

"We do. But I'd rather walk into headquarters with some idea of where things stand regarding the trial. I don't have a phone or a laptop or any way to access the internet. But libraries have computers that anyone can use, free of charge."

"Couldn't you wait until we get to Madison and borrow your friend's iPad?"

"I could. But I'd rather get some of this straight before our arrival. And I'd like to keep Alice's involvement in this as minimal as possible."

Minimal? Isobel expelled a short breath through her nose. Didn't Jimmy realize that taking care of a nine-month-old child was not minimal at all, but a major favor to ask of a friend? Annoyed on Alice's behalf as well as her own, she bit back a retort and settled against the seat.

The scenery along the interstate began to change the farther east they drove though Wisconsin. The rolling hills in the western part of the state leveled out as flat, harvested fields stretched for miles against an azure sky. It was calming to watch the dappled horses and cattle grazing a few yards away from farmhouse doors. As they approached the town of Tomah, the landscape shifted again as rocky cliffs jutted through the pines on either side of the highway. Jimmy flicked on the turn signal and, a moment later, they were following signs to the library.

He pulled in next to a two-story brick building. "Want to grab Calvin and come in with me?"

"No. I'll just hang here. Maybe see if Calvin wants to nurse, though it hasn't been that long since we left the hotel." A sudden thought popped into her head. "You don't have a library card. Won't you need to show some sort of ID?"

He ran his fingers through his close-cropped hair. "I'm hoping they offer guest passes like they do back home. It shouldn't take long. Fifteen minutes tops. I'll leave the keys in the ignition in case you get cold."

"We'll be fine," she insisted. After all, the sun was out and the temperature was warmer than it had been the night before. In fact, it was practically balmy. She watched as Jimmy jogged toward the bright red door. She hoped for his sake that he was right about not needing to show his ID.

As soon as Jimmy disappeared into the library, Isobel moved to the back to sit next to Calvin. "Want me to take that?" she asked, reaching for the bit of bagel still clutched in his fist. His indignant yelp proved that he wanted no such thing. Her boy sure had a mind of his own these days. In so many ways, he was acting so grown up, though it did sound silly to describe a nine-month-old that way. But he had changed so much in the weeks since they had arrived at the safe house. He had started to scoot and to pull himself upright on the furniture. And he seemed to understand simple words and commands, though he seemed less inclined to obey.

She had actually found herself feeling sorry that Ricky would miss so many milestones of Calvin's life. It didn't make any sense that she should care one bit about a man who tried to kill her and kidnap her baby. She knew that. Still, it was hard not to feel sad to imagine a father never getting to hold his little boy.

Her dad would have a field day analyzing what it all meant. He'd claim that her concern about Ricky was a smokescreen for a yearning for her old life and the perks of being married to a wealthy man. "No more lifestyles of the rich and famous for you." That was what he'd said when she'd called to tell him that she had finalized her divorce.

But hadn't she proved that she was made of sterner stuff in building a new life for herself and her son in Dagger

Lake? It hadn't been easy. Though she was still living in a small apartment, she had decorated a little room for Calvin with a wide shelf with all his favorite books and toys. Studying the Bible helped keep her centered as well, as did good friends at church and at the bank where she worked. Sure, she had made mistakes, but didn't everyone? Did that make her damaged goods?

A crackling of tires against gravel marked the arrival of a police car in the lot just a few feet away. The uniformed driver took his time stepping out of his vehicle, his hand lingering close to his holster. Instinctively, Isobel slumped down in her seat.

Was he looking for her? And/or for Jimmy, who was probably sitting in an open carrel inside the library? If only she could warn him. But how?

She reached for the Bible in her bag, opened it to Psalms and began to read. But she couldn't concentrate.

She tucked in a marker and slipped it back into her bag. She needed to stay calm. There were any number of reasons why a police officer had showed up in this particular parking lot. Reasons that had nothing whatsoever to do with what had happened back at the first hotel. She was becoming paranoid, that's what it was. Fearful of her own shadow.

But just in case, she kept her eyes fixed straight ahead as she whispered a prayer for Jimmy.

NINE

The waiting and watching were the worst. Ricky had always mocked her for being scared of her own shadow. And even after the policeman climbed back into his car and pulled out of the lot, Isobel continued to fret, turning her head and tapping her fingers as fifteen more minutes passed without any sign of Jimmy. She could only imagine what was happening inside—voices raised in anger as Jimmy was escorted to a back room by security and charged with failing to produce a proper ID.

Did public libraries even have security guards on staff? She hadn't been inside one for years, so she really couldn't say. Still, Jimmy had been gone for—she checked the clock on the dash—twenty-seven minutes. Time to go inside and check out the situation for herself.

But as she was reaching around to unsnap Calvin from his car seat, Jimmy bounded out the door and down the pathway toward the car. She climbed back into the front seat as Jimmy slid in beside her. Moments later, they were back on the interstate.

After several minutes of strained silence, she trusted herself to speak. "Did you have a problem getting on the internet?"

Jimmy shook his head. "Nope. They have passes like I thought."

"So, what did you find out about the trial?"

"It's going ahead. I didn't have time to do much more than scan the headlines."

"What about Stephanie? Was there anything about her being killed in a raid on the safe house?"

"Like I said, I didn't do a complete overview. I loaded most of what I found on the thumb drive attached to my key chain. When we get to Alice's, we can take a look."

"It took you awfully long to copy a few files."

"It was crazy busy. I had to wait a while for an open computer. I was going to come out and explain, but I saw that cop through the window. So it seemed best to chill inside."

"I suppose the fact that they seem to be moving forward without me is proof that they have enough evidence to get a conviction. Of course, my testimony would be a lot more powerful if they let me talk about what happened last winter when Ricky tried to kidnap Calvin and blow up the bank with me in it. But Stephanie said it would be inadmissible if we tried to bring any of that up in the federal case in Detroit."

"Well, she's the expert. And the prosecution team must feel confident about the other witnesses they have lined up to testify against Ricky. Which begs the question—why the attempt to take you out?"

"Ricky's goal is to get Calvin. It always has been, and always will be. That's how he thinks, Jimmy."

"Still, I wonder if there isn't more behind this than a father trying to kidnap his son. Something we're missing. Something personal to you."

"He wants me dead. That's as personal as you can get."

"Right. But it still seems like there may be another agenda in play."

She huffed out a sigh of impatience. She was done talking about this. But when Jimmy quirked a brow, her face warmed with embarrassment. She shouldn't get upset when he was just trying to help. "Wow. I should know better than to try to hide my emotions from a trained therapist."

"Don't worry. I'm still a guy, so I probably miss most of that stuff."

Isobel twisted her head toward the window to hide the amused smile forming on her lips. She was coming to realize that Jimmy really did have a sense of humor, which was a trait he had kept under wraps at the safe house.

A glance out the window revealed a landscape that was shifting once again. Tall pines pressed close to the sides of the road as they passed through the Dells, which countless billboards promoted as a waterpark wonderland.

"Looks like a fun place. Maybe I'll bring Calvin here when he gets older. Sorry if I was rude before with all the questions, by the way. I was worried when I saw that cop standing there waiting. I thought maybe the marshals had put out some sort of APB on us. Maybe they think you're the mole working for Ricky."

Jimmy shot her a look. "I assume when they picked up Ryan, he was able to give an account of the raid, at least as much as he had witnessed."

"But you said it could be anybody, remember? Ryan thought it was Len."

"I did hear him say that, Isobel, but that doesn't make it true. And if anyone thought I was working for Ricky, why would I have rescued you at the safe house? It's confusing. But at some point, I'll figure it out." He pointed to a green sign announcing the first of four exits to Madison. "According to my calculations, we're less than fifteen minutes from our destination."

"Maybe you should give me a quick rundown of who's who in the household."

Jimmy nodded. "There's Alice and her husband, Patrick. Five kids, not sure of their ages. Alice was a teacher before starting to home school. I seem to remember that she likes to cook, but that could be just wishful thinking on my part."

Isobel suddenly felt sheepish. While waiting at the library, she had finished the bagels from the hotel. And Jimmy hadn't eaten anything since breakfast. She fished around in her purse for the smashed protein bar. It was looking even worse for the wear, but it was better than nothing.

"Want this?" she asked.

He laughed. "Tempting, but maybe later." He signaled a turn as they skirted the white dome of the capitol building and headed south through the town.

Two more right turns later, they pulled to the curb in front of a ranch-style house in the middle of the block. "Here we are. Ready to go?"

"As ready as I'll ever be to ask for help from someone I don't know and who you haven't seen or talked to for a half dozen years."

But as it turned out, showing up on the doorstep of the Cullen house was a lot less awkward than Isobel had expected. Alice greeted Jimmy with a tight hug, claiming to be excited to see him. And she didn't act the least bit bothered when she realized that his entourage included a strange woman and a nine-month-old kid. Even better, she didn't even flinch when Jimmy mentioned his plan to leave Calvin in her care for a few days.

"It won't be a problem," Alice insisted. "The older girls

will help out. Now that Johnny is six, we all miss having a baby." She shot Patrick, her husband, a pointed look.

Alice asked a lot of questions—about Jimmy's job and his sister Meg and what his family was up to back home. While they talked, her kids were everywhere, alternately acting shy and bombarding Jimmy with questions about his duties as a marshal.

Dinner was meatloaf and mashed potatoes. Alice apologized for the simple fare, but no one was complaining, least of all Jimmy, who didn't need to be persuaded to have a second helping of everything. A porta-crib was unearthed from the basement and set up in the playroom at the top of the stairs.

"The kids usually read in their rooms before bed. They're reasonably quiet, but I hope the excitement won't be too much for Calvin," Alice said as she led Isobel up the stairs.

"He's usually a good sleeper. I'll leave you the formula I have in my bag. He prefers to nurse, but he's been pretty good with taking the bottle. Once his belly is full, he'll be good for seven or eight hours at least."

But it took longer than expected to settle her little boy down. By the time she rejoined the adults in the living room, Jimmy was wrapping up an edited version of what had happened at the safe house.

"So, yeah," he said, leaning back against the couch cushions. "Our goal is to get Isobel to Detroit so she can testify and put this whole thing to rest."

Patrick pressed for information about the specific charges being brought against Ricky.

Jimmy pulled the thumb drive out of his pocket and held it up. "I'm hoping to find some answers on this. So far, I've just read the headlines and short blurbs about the case."

"Let's take a look then," Patrick said, reaching for a laptop and opening it up.

Alice motioned that Isobel should follow her into the kitchen where she put a kettle on to boil and set a handful of lemon teabags in a basket on the table.

"I can't believe that story about the tracker in your son's stuffed bear," she said, pouring hot water into two mugs and setting one in front of Isobel. "To know that they'd take something so innocent and violate it like that must have broken you in a way I can only imagine."

Isobel unwrapped a lemon lift teabag and dropped it into her cup. The discovery of the tracker had hardly been the worst of it, but Alice didn't need to hear the details. Best to keep it light, at least for the moment. "It was a blessing that we found it when we did. And Jimmy's been a rock. I don't know what we would have done without him."

Alice pulled in a long breath. "He's a good guy, that's for sure. Have you met his sister Meg?" Isobel shook her head. "I suppose that was a silly question, given that you didn't know Jimmy until he was assigned to protect you. When you do meet her, she can tell you the story about how Jimmy put his life on hold to take care of the younger kids in the family after his parents were killed in a car accident."

Isobel widened her eyes. "He never said anything about that."

"Yeah. It was tragic. Jimmy was a freshman at Harvard and had set his sights on becoming a surgeon when a drunk driver plowed into his mom and dad's SUV. With three younger kids still needing care, he transferred to a local college close to home, stepping up as both mom and dad to all three of his siblings while working and going to school part-time. Meg said he never once complained about any of it. Actually, I'm not surprised that all of this never came up in conversation. He likes to keep the personal stuff close to the vest."

Isobel nodded. "I noticed that, too. He will answer questions, though sometimes in a cryptic way."

"Did he tell you about Kim?" Alice paused then grimaced. "I can see by the look on your face that he didn't. I probably shouldn't have mentioned her either. Let's do something more proactive. Like finding you some toiletries and clothing you'll need for the rest of your journey."

"Thank you. You have been amazing with all of this. But I do feel like I need to address something you said before when you were talking about Jimmy's sister. You seemed to imply that, at some point, I'd get to meet her. But it's not like that between me and Jimmy. Once I testify in Detroit, he'll move on to his next assignment. And Calvin and I will go home to North Dakota."

Alice smiled. "Maybe. But keep an open mind because I really do think you might be wrong about that."

Jimmy lifted his gaze from the screen of the laptop, distracted by the sound of shuffling up and down the stairs.

"What are they doing?" he asked Patrick.

"No idea." Patrick slipped on his glasses to read a section of small print from the newspaper article about the trial. "Honestly, Jimmy, none of this makes sense. Assuming the veracity of this article you copied from yesterday's *Free Press*, the defense is making mincemeat of the prosecution's witnesses. This so-called whistleblower, who's one of Bashir's main accountants, seems to have been completely worthless in proving any of the RICO charges in the case. His big moment on the stand involved describing Bashir as a dedicated philanthropist. How did they not anticipate what he'd say under questioning? And he's not the only one. Given that they've already called half a dozen witnesses, they haven't proved anything beyond a reasonable doubt. I'm surprised the defense hasn't moved for a directed verdict."

"Do you think the judge would grant it?"

"I don't see why not. Unless the prosecution has something more up their sleeves. Even if Isobel can place Bashir at the scene and establish a direct connection, it still seems weak if they're hoping for a conviction. Especially given the fact that there's a much stronger case waiting to be brought in North Dakota. I wish I could understand what the thinking was here. If I didn't know better, I'd say that someone wants this whole thing to go away."

Jimmy tented his arms and cradled his head against them. "I thought from the beginning that Isobel was a pawn in some sort of game in the prosecution team's game."

"Can you trust your boss at least?"

"I think so." He thought for a minute. "No, I take that back. I am sure I can."

Patrick nodded. "Then my advice would be not to worry about anything but keeping her safe."

Keeping her safe. All along, that had been the main goal of his assignment. And so far, despite all the forces working against them, he had done his best. But the challenges they were facing were not over yet. And he was starting to realize that until Ricky Bashir was convicted, they never would be.

Patrick had given him a lot to think about. But it was late, and he was finding it a challenge to keep all the new information straight in his head. So when Isobel and Alice rejoined them in the living room, clutching bed linens and blankets to their chests, Jimmy took the cue that it was time for bed.

"Isobel can stay in the guest room," Alice declared. "And, Jimmy, if you don't mind, you can bunk in the den."

"Sounds like a plan." Jimmy stretched as he pushed himself upright from the couch. "I didn't realize how tired I was until I stood up. Thank you both for everything. I only hope that I can someday find a way to repay the debt."

He headed into the den where Alice had already opened the sleeper sofa and made up the bed. And despite a rather long metal rod under the mattress, it was the best night's sleep he'd had in days—with the added bonus of waking up to the sound of happy laughter and the tantalizing aroma of bacon wafting through the room.

But before anything else, propriety required a quick shower and a change into the clothing Alice had thoughtfully left in his room. Patrick's jeans and flannel shirt were a good fit, though perhaps a bit too hip to suit his usual style. He wasn't complaining, though. All he felt was overwhelming gratitude toward the Cullens.

Isobel was already awake when he came into the kitchen and so was Calvin, who was banging his fist on the high chair next to the table. He suppressed a smile at the sight of the new outfit Isobel was sporting, courtesy of Alice: black exercise pants with a stylish top, her hair pulled back in a loose ponytail. She looked like a model.

But with two opinionated younger sisters as a guide, he had learned early that it was never a good idea to comment on a woman's appearance, even if his reaction was positive, though apparently, the rule didn't apply the other way around.

"I like your new look," Isobel said.

Alice stuck her head out of what appeared to be a pantry door. "He does look extremely handsome. Help yourself to coffee, Jimmy. I'm planning to whip up some eggs and toast for breakfast."

Moments later, the rest of the clan drifted in to join them—Patrick, followed by his two daughters and his three sons.

"Grab some cereal and take it into the sunroom." Alice issued orders with the skill of a drill sergeant. "Math test today for all of you, except the littles."

The kids followed their mom's instructions, leaving the adults to enjoy a quiet breakfast without any more questions about shoot-outs and bad guys.

"We'll hit the road as soon as we finish breakfast," Jimmy promised while spooning another scoop of scrambled eggs onto his plate. "Our visit has caused more than a few disruptions to your routine."

"It really and truly is our pleasure," Alice claimed. She set her fork down and leaned forward on the table. "Anyway, Patrick and I are glad to have a quiet moment to talk to you about your plans for the next few days."

"Correct," Patrick chimed in. "Alice and I talked last night, and we agreed that we want to help in any way we can. One of the ideas we had was to buy you tickets for the ferry to Michigan. It would be safer and faster than driving through Chicago and a lot more restful given the out-of-control traffic through the city."

"I need to stop you there," Jimmy interrupted. "We appreciate the offer. But you've done enough already by feeding us, putting us up for the night and agreeing to care for Calvin."

"I told you," Alice said. "Watching an adorable nine-month-old is a treat. But let's talk about the ferry. It leaves from Milwaukee, and you can park the car on the lower deck and enjoy the ride. Don't you think it's a brilliant plan?"

Jimmy shook his head. "I assume we would need to show our IDs before they let us board."

Alice graced him with a smug smile. "We thought about that. You can use our driver's licenses to get past the check-point. We've taken the ferry to our cabin in Ludington, and they never do more than glance at IDs. And take this as you like, but both of you look enough like us to pass muster."

"But won't you need your licenses to drive?" Isobel asked.

"Nah." Patrick dismissed her concern with a wave of his hand. "If they question you, just claim it's all a mis-take. But that's not going to happen. And if need be, you can stop for the night at our vacation home in Ludington, though it's an hour north in the opposite direction. But it will be nice not having to deal with checking into a motel."

Jimmy looked at Isobel. Was she on board with this crazy notion of masquerading as the Cullens and riding the ferry? She didn't look opposed to the idea, that was for sure. She was smiling and looking kind of teary-eyed at the gesture. He got that. He felt a bit misty-eyed himself as he considered the generosity of two people who had offered so much assistance purely out of the kindness of their hearts.

Isobel met his glance and nodded.

"I think it might work, Jimmy," she said.

Would it?

The thought continued to boomerang around in his head, even as Patrick went online to check if there was still space available for a twelve-thirty departure that very afternoon.

There was, and without pausing to revisit the pros and cons of the plan, the booking was made, which meant they had less than four hours to drive to Milwaukee and get on board. Suddenly, it was a rush to pack up and take their leave, Isobel's lips quivering as she held her little son for what might be the last time for several days. Jimmy could tell that she was determined not to cry, at least not in front of the Cullens.

Patrick helped him carry their belongings to the car, along with a laptop he had insisted on lending them. As they stood in the driveway, saying goodbye, Patrick pressed an envelope into his hand.

"Open this later when you're on the way," he said.

Isobel kept it together as he pulled away from the curb. But when they reached the stop sign at the end of the road, he could see the teardrops falling from her eyes. As he reached into the pocket of his shirt for a tissue, his fingers brushed against the envelope from Patrick.

"Want to open this and see what's inside?"

She nodded.

Out of the corner of his eye, he watched as she tore open the envelope and unfolded the note inside. "It's the address of their place in Ludington. And the code for the front door, along with instructions for accessing the internet, which are on the bulletin board in the kitchen."

"But that's not all." Isobel's eyes glistened with tears as she held up what she had what she had found at the bottom of the envelope—six neatly folded fifty-dollar bills.

TEN

It took a mighty effort for Isobel to pretend to be okay about leaving Calvin with the Cullens in Madison. Nothing against Alice and Patrick, but the longest she had been separated from her little boy had been during that horrible night when he was born. She could still recall the terror of not knowing where he was as she'd waited at the hospital, hoping and praying that Ricky had not succeeded in kidnapping their son. It had been the longest night of her life.

And now she was once again entrusting Calvin to someone else's care while Ricky's men remained on the hunt. A shiver ran down her spine and she pulled her body tighter in its half-sitting, half-curled position in the front seat as she looked out the window.

"Don't worry, Isabel. Calvin will be safe with Alice," Jimmy reassured her. "And this will be over soon."

Isobel shrugged, but didn't turn her head. If only that were true. But Jimmy didn't know what Ricky was capable of. Sure, he had read the file and knew her backstory. But words on paper could never capture the ruthlessness and cunning of Ricky Bashir.

Jimmy's eyes were full of sympathy as he turned to face her. "I don't mean to sugar coat what you've been through already or any of the challenges that lie ahead. I know none of this is going to be simple. Maybe when we get on the ferry, we can fire up the computer and get an update on what's happening in the courtroom."

She nodded. She appreciated Jimmy's concern, but right now she didn't feel like talking about the trial. In fact, she didn't want to think about Ricky at all. She just wanted to concentrate her thoughts on her sweet baby boy, to imagine his chipmunk cheeks and big blue eyes and wonder what he was doing. Probably having a grand time, surrounded by a gaggle of kids.

"How about some music?" Jimmy once again interrupted her musings. "I've mostly stopped listening to the radio because I can't stand most of the modern stuff they play. But maybe I can find an oldies country station."

Isobel could feel her lips crease into a smile. Jimmy's curmudgeonly attitude didn't quite match the hipster attire he had borrowed from Patrick.

"Yeah, you can laugh," he said. "But I'm telling you, music was at its very best during the nineties and early two thousands. You're probably way too young to remember all the classic Toby Keith and Alan Jackson songs."

"Hey, I was born in the nineties!"

"Born in the nineties. Good grief, you're making me feel ancient."

Isobel would have reacted to Jimmy's comment, but she could hear a smile in his voice. She suspected he was exaggerating his remarks about music and her age to lighten the mood and to stop her from thinking about Calvin. And it certainly was true that she had been born in the nineties. Barely—1999. But still.

Not that age really mattered. She had been twenty-one when she'd met Ricky, yet she might as well have been fifteen, given the lack of experience and worldliness she had brought into that relationship. But she had grown up a lot in the ensuing years. She had come to realize that age was just a number.

"How old are you?" She decided to play along and enjoy the distraction. She turned her head away from the window to get a better look at the marshal.

True, there were some lines around his eyes. She had noticed how they crinkled whenever he laughed or smiled. And maybe there was a little silver mixed in his hair, but it was so light that it was barely noticeable. He was obviously one of those people who stayed in good shape no matter what. If she had to guess, she'd put his age at about thirty-five. Maybe younger.

Jimmy shot her an amused smile. "Let's just say that I've got a decade on you, and then some."

So she was close. Late thirties. That was a good age for a man.

"I didn't realize therapists were allowed to listen to country music. I thought it had to always be Mozart and Mueller."

"Hey now, don't be throwing shade at classical music. I love that, too."

Isobel couldn't help herself. She had to laugh. "So, which is your favorite?"

Jimmy's mouth twisted up in a wry smile. "In all seriousness? Both. Growing up, I loved country. My brother used to give me a hard time because he preferred hip-hop."

"Your brother?" She continued to be curious about Jimmy's past, especially after her conversation with Alice.

"Yeah, my brother. Along with Meg and Carly, my youngest sisters. I've got a family, just like everybody else. But hey, look! There's a sign for the ferry. It says we're only ten minutes away."

Isobel glanced up at a billboard with big block letters.
AVOID THE CHICAGO TRAFFIC!
SIT BACK AND ENJOY THE BEAUTIFUL LAKE
VIEW!
MILWAUKEE TO MUSKEGON.
TAKE THE NEXT EXIT AND FOLLOW SIGNS!

A heavy weight plummeted in Isobel's stomach. No, no,
no. This couldn't be happening.

"We need to turn around."

"What?"

"We can't take the ferry."

"Why not?"

Jimmy flicked on his turn signal and cast a concerned
expression her way. "Tell me what's wrong. And then we
can decide if we want to change course. At this point, we're
not committed. Just let me know what suddenly upset you."

Isobel swallowed and then counted to ten silently in her
head to calm her pounding heart. "I didn't know that the
ferry went to Muskegon."

"Yeah. We dock at Muskegon and, from there, we'll
drive east to Detroit. Why is that a problem?"

Isobel clenched her fingers together. Seriously, did
Jimmy think she was an idiot and didn't know basic geog-
raphy? She might not have an advanced degree like him,
but she understood the basics. "I know where Detroit is.
I just didn't realize that we'd be stopping in Muskegon…
That's where Ricky was born and raised. And a lot of his
family still live there."

"Okay." Jimmy's voice was measured as he continued to
follow the signs to the ferry. "I understand being freaked
out that we're headed to Ricky's hometown. But do you
know for a fact that his relatives are criminals?"

"I actually do." Isobel tried to keep her voice steady, but

Jimmy's style of questioning felt patronizing. "Ricky told me about his family when we first got married. He claimed that he had gotten involved in dealing drugs because of them. But he had walked away from all that and moved to Detroit. Of course, he didn't tell me that starting over just meant building his own criminal enterprise in a new city." Isobel could hear the bitterness in her voice.

"Okay." Jimmy drummed his fingers along the steering wheel. "I understand the potential problem here. But I think we should still go forward with the plan. If we turn around now, we've wasted a lot of time and may miss the chance to testify, and we'll have to go through Chicago. From what Patrick told me last night, the traffic there is stop-and-go all the way through. Bashir's crime network also extends there, and we could just as likely to be spotted driving through the city as taking the ferry. Being seen on the ferry would make us sitting ducks, but the journey is quicker. We'll be off the boat and headed toward Detroit in half the time."

Isobel clenched her lips and sighed. The desire to scream out in frustration bubbled up inside her. Of course, heading through Chicago was a huge risk. And time was running out with the trial already in progress. They couldn't afford any more delays.

"We need to think about this rationally," Jimmy said, pointing to the line of cars forming in front of them. "First of all, our tickets are under different names. And second, so are our IDs. As a simple precaution, you can just slide down low in the seat, so no one will even notice you at the point of entry."

"Okay." It was hard to argue with his logic. And as far as she knew, Ricky didn't have relatives working on the ferry. Even if he did, how likely was it that she would be recognized based on meeting her once at the wedding?

And even if she was spotted, it would have to be by someone willing to pass along the information to Ricky's associates. And from everything she had been led to understand, a number of members of the Bashir clan were currently not on speaking terms with each other.

The likelihood of encountering a problem was next to nothing.

So why did she feel so uneasy as the car inched forward in the line toward the ferry?

"Tickets please," an officious voice demanded.

Jimmy passed a folded printout through the open window. The official scanned the barcode on the document and handed it back. A moment later, he motioned for Jimmy to drive up the concrete slope. So far, so good.

Isobel slumped down in her seat as Jimmy steered the Camaro toward the row of open spaces on the bottom deck. A dark green van pulled into a spot directly behind them. Isobel flinched and then relaxed as half a dozen kids poured out through the sliding door.

"I think this is where we get out, too." Jimmy shifted into Park and twisted the key out of the ignition.

Isobel slid upright and gazed at her surroundings. The Camaro was the second in a line already about twelve vehicles deep. She glanced at Jimmy, who seemed to be watching her, his mouth curled into a questioning slant.

"Ready?"

She nodded and stepped out of the car.

"We'll leave the laptop behind for now. I think we need a break from talking about the case. If we change our minds, we can always come back and get it. For now, let's find a place to get some coffee." Jimmy was already weaving his way through a row of cars.

Isobel took a deep breath and followed him up two sets of stairs to the upper deck. The lake was surprisingly calm with just a bit of choppiness when the wind blew. She could feel Jimmy's eyes, watching the crowd as he stood beside her, and she wondered, not for the first time, if he was regretting his assignment to her case.

But he did seem to be smiling, so maybe everything really was going to be all right. As she watched the waves lap over the ramp, the tension across her back and neck began to ease and she started to relax.

"Uh, Isobel." Jimmy's voice was suddenly close to her ear. "Don't turn around, but someone on the lower deck seems to be staring in our direction. I'll tell you when he looks away and then you can see if you recognize him."

The knots that had begun to loosen retied themselves across her shoulders. She closed her eyes, pressed her lips together and waited.

"Okay, he's pulled out his phone and is staring at the screen. Check him out. The big, burly guy by the green sedan."

Isobel swiveled her head and surveyed the scene, taking in the rows of cars and ferry workers in their bright orange vests. Her eyes darted, searching for a green vehicle with the man standing beside it. There! She saw him, half turned to the side with a phone pressed to his ear. She squinted. Did she recognize him? It was hard to tell from this angle.

Another worker walked by and engaged the man in conversation, causing him to turn slightly, revealing more than just his profile.

Her stomach recoiled with nausea as powerful as a cresting wave.

"I take it you know him," Jimmy said after quickly reading the expression on her face.

"That's Ricky's first cousin—Marty. We need to get off this boat immediately."

A surge of protectiveness swelled in his chest, and without even realizing what he was doing, Jimmy wrapped his arm around Isobel's shoulders, pulling her tight to shield her from this new, looming threat. He flexed his fingers and blew out a breath from between his teeth—a sharp kick of anger flexing through his senses.

He could feel Isobel's face pressed against his rib cage. He suspected that she was crying. Not that he could blame her. Ricky Bashir's influence was a lot more far-reaching than he had ever imagined. And now that they were getting closer to Detroit, the net was closing in on them. Who had Marty been talking to on the phone? And who or what would be waiting for them when they disembarked in Muskegon?

He had no way of knowing. And that meant planning for the worst-case scenario.

"Look," he whispered against Isobel's downturned head, "they've closed the ramp, so they're not going to let anyone disembark at the moment. We'd call more attention to ourselves if we tried. And we'd need to leave the car, so that would be a problem. At this point, we can't be sure if Marty actually recognized you. It may be that he didn't and there's nothing to worry about." He took a step away and looked into Isobel's eyes. Sure enough, they were damp with tears. "And even if he did spot you, we still have the advantage. He doesn't know that we're onto him. So that gives us time to plan what to do when the ferry docks in Michigan."

"You don't think he'll try something on the boat?" Isobel's eyes had a hopeful shimmer.

He rolled his head back on his shoulders. "He could. But why would he? There would be a lot of witnesses. And he's just one person."

"Ladies and gentlemen." A voice crackled from the speakers above them. "We are experiencing a minor technical issue, which will result in a short delay. We are sorry for any inconvenience. We will update you with new information as needed. Thank you in advance for your patience."

A delay? Jimmy resisted the impulse to punch the guardrail in frustration. He should have listened when Isobel had told him not to board the ferry. Now they were essentially sitting ducks, trapped for the next two hours, or longer, given the uncertain length of the delay. His brain shifted through all the possible ways this could go down, desperate to determine the best possible course of action to keep Isobel safe. Find a place to hole up or hide in plain sight among the other passengers? Go back to the car?

"Jimmy." Isobel's voice cut through his thoughts. "What's going on?"

He shook his head. "I'm not sure. But I don't like it. There could be a real technical issue with the ferry. Or—" he shrugged "—it could be something else."

"Something else? Like Marty arranging for backup in the form of more men?"

"That's what I'm afraid of. But we still have the upper hand here. They don't realize we're aware of what's going on." He hoped he sounded more optimistic than he felt. "Let's find a place with a view of the ramp and talk through our options."

He took Isobel's hand and led her to the other side of the upper deck. There was a family nearby, but not so close that they could hear their conversation. He huddled close to her, keeping his eyes focused on the lift bridge connecting the boat to the dock.

"The way I see it, we have two different problems. What might happen on the boat and what awaits us in Muskegon. And remember, there is still the possibility that nothing will come of any of this. But it's best to be prepared."

He glanced at Isobel. She nodded.

"Okay. If the ramp is lowered for any late arrivals, you'll need to hide. It doesn't matter where—the bathroom or as part of another family, as long as you stay within the public areas of the boat. I'll deal with Marty and whoever else shows up."

"But—" Isobel began to interrupt, but he held up his hand.

"This next part is critical. When it's time to disembark, you get in the Camaro and drive as far away from the port as quickly as you can. If I'm not there when you get to the car, that doesn't change anything. You drive. Don't wait for me."

"What if I want to wait? Isn't that my choice?"

"Yes, but we need to be strategic. And the best option is to get you out of town as quickly as you can."

"I hear you, but your point is overruled. After everything we've been through together, they're not going to split us up now. Let's just decide on a spot where we can meet on the shore."

Jimmy could feel his lips twitch up into a half smile. He appreciated her faith in his ability to deal with Marty, though he wasn't quite so optimistic about the outcome of such a match. But it was clear by the set of Isobel's jaw that she wasn't giving in.

"Okay. Fine. I agree, with one caveat. When you get off the ferry, you can't hang around on shore and wait for me. You should drive two miles north until you find a spot where you can pull over and wait. But if I don't show up in twenty minutes, you head straight for the federal court-house in Detroit."

Beside him, he heard Isobel sniffle, but he didn't turn his head. He couldn't watch her cry again. It broke his heart.

"Look." Isobel raised her hand to point, but he reached over and pulled it down, curling her fingers closed.

A black Suburban was making its way along the dock. As the driver inched forward, Jimmy's heartrate steadily increased its tempo in his chest. Initially, there seemed to be some sort of disagreement with the ticket clerk. But just as he allowed himself to believe that his fears were unfounded, the doors on the vehicle opened and two men began to walk toward the boat, leaving the Suburban be-hind. Apparently, there hadn't been a parking spot on the ferry. But there was room for two more passengers. Jimmy followed the action as a small side ramp was lowered for the men. From the bruises on their face, it wasn't hard to recognize them as the two assailants from the hotel.

ELEVEN

Go time. For one fleeting moment, Jimmy considered grabbing Isobel's hand and jumping off the ferry.

But it was a bad idea, for any number of reasons, most of all because the laptop in their car could definitely be traced to the Cullens.

But hiding on board was a temporary solution at best. There was also the issue of a likely greeting party on the other side of the lake. It'd only taken Ricky's cousin a half hour to get two men to the ferry in Milwaukee. With his family connections, he could easily arrange for a nice little army to await their arrival in Muskegon. Recent events certainly suggested that the Bashir family seemed to have the ferry company deep in their pocket.

Could Isobel sense the regret he was feeling at not heeding her earlier warning? Maybe. Her eyes remained focused on the lakeshore, which was getting smaller and smaller as they moved out into the deeper waters. There was something so fragile and vulnerable in the way she clenched the guardrail, as if holding on tight would shield her from the enemy lurking close by.

"Isobel," he whispered.

As she turned to face him, his heart somersaulted in his chest. He'd expected fresh tears shining in her eyes, but what he saw instead was the gleam of anger and determination. This was a woman who wasn't about to go down without a fight. It was impossible not to admire her courage and grit.

"Isobel." He tried again, his voice sounding thick over the lump in his throat. "It's not safe for you to be out in the open. We have to find a place for you to hide."

"What about you? Those men saw you at the hotel. You're in danger, too."

"I'm going to assume that, at this point, I'm not on their radar. And I have a weapon, if worse comes to worst. Besides, you're the one they're looking for."

With a barely perceptible movement of her chin, she nodded her agreement.

He considered the places where she could take cover. The most obvious was the restroom. There, she would be out of sight, but not completely alone. But if the men couldn't find her among the other passengers, surely that would be the first place they would look. Another idea struck him—she could hide in the car. But Marty could easily find an excuse to check on the vehicles. And if they found Isobel there, no one would be around to help her.

There had to be a better option.

Jimmy scanned first to the left and then to the right. The third-floor deck had an open-air shade top. Great for surveillance. Not great for hiding. Just around the corner from the bathrooms was a white door with a little red cross.

He did another quick scan of the area. So far, the three men on the deck below were sticking together, systematically surveying the crowd and wandering through the larger throngs of people. It was only a matter of time before they expanded their search. Slipping his hand into Isobel's, he led her toward the red cross that marked the first-aid office.

"Excuse me," he said to the female attendant who appeared in the open doorway. "My friend here is feeling seasick. Could she get a patch of something, and maybe lie down for a bit?"

"Sure," the girl agreed, pushing her wire-rimmed glasses up toward the bridge of her nose. "The lake is relatively calm today, but sometimes just being on water is enough to throw off our equilibrium. I can place this patch here on your arm, and you'll feel better real soon."

"Thank you," Isobel mumbled, shooting Jimmy a questioning glance.

"Also," Jimmy added, "this is kind of a big ask, but do you by any chance have an extra shirt and hat? Maybe in the lost and found? My friend—" he pointed at Isobel "—would never complain, but she sometimes gets migraines. If she could borrow a light jacket and a hat to shield her from the sun, it would help."

Beside him, Isobel gave a slight moan.

"Yeah, yeah, I totally get it." The attendant nodded. "My sister gets horrible headaches, too. Let me check and see if we have anything that will fit."

A moment later, she reappeared from a back closet with a bundle in her arms.

"I couldn't find T-shirts or hats. But how about a windbreaker? It has a hood. Not that it will offer much shade. But if you pull it tight, the pressure will help with the headache." She thrust a red jacket into Isobel's hands.

"Great! And thank you so much." Jimmy began to back away toward the door. "I'll step outside while she lies down."

He ducked out of the first-aid office and checked around the vicinity. No sign of the three men. With four quick strides, he was back at the guardrail. He peered down at the crowd on the lower level. Where was Marty, and where were the men who had arrived in the Suburban? They seemed to have split up, which was all the better. It would be easier to take them on one at time.

As he'd suspected, Marty was on the lower deck, walking along the rows of cars and peering into each. The scrawnier of the two late arrivals leaned against the concession stand, surveying the scene on the second level. But where was perp number three? Jimmy shifted his gaze to once again scrutinize the deck in front of him. There were a couple of families sitting in booths, looking out at the lake. A gaggle of teenage girls had gathered on the opposite side of the boat. Two middle-aged women were emerging from the bathroom, and an older man stood off to the side by himself.

Jimmy reached under his shirt where he had tucked his gun. Locked and loaded, just in case.

He hesitated for a moment as he considered his next step. Should he try going back down to the second level? But it would be a risky move, without first knowing where the third man was. A sudden movement caught his eye and he swiveled his head just in time to see someone climbing the stairs. Turning his back, he swiveled again, keeping his head tilted at an angle to allow him to watch what was happening on deck number three.

For the span of one heartbeat, he waited and then saw the man he had fought in the stairwell just two nights earlier now climbing the stairs. The large man, sporting a purplish bruise along his temple and below his left eye, cast a cursory glance over the passengers.

Would he recognize him? Apparently not. After a moment's hesitation, the man began to walk toward the bathroom. He stopped at the door marked Women and slipped inside.

Jimmy waited a moment and then followed behind.

The motion of the door opening and closing was caught in the mirror hanging over the sink. Alerted to his presence, the man stepped out of an open stall, turned and started to reach for his gun. But Jimmy was ready. Diving headfirst, he pinned the man's arms in a waist-high tackle. Knocked off balance, his adversary swayed sideways and then crashed to the floor. Jimmy sprang up and shook the pistol from his opponent's grip. He realized with a start that the man wasn't moving. The fall onto the hard tiled floor had knocked him out cold.

Jimmy acted quickly to remove the man's sweatshirt, using the sleeves to tie his assailant's hands together behind his back. He picked up the fallen pistol and tossed it into a trash can next to the wall. Then, he pulled the man into the stall, kicked the door closed and locked it, then slithered out through the opening below.

One down, two to go.

And with firepower to spare.

Less than two minutes had passed since he'd entered the bathroom, but it felt much longer as he exited through the swinging door. Once again, he checked the whereabouts of the other two men. Both were roughly in the same area he'd last seen them.

Could he take the stairs down to the next level without being spotted? Because as long as he could maintain the element of surprise, he had the upper hand.

He rubbed his hands across his jaw, considering the risk, when one of the nearby families stood up and began to make their way to the lower level. That was his cue. He hurried up behind them, blending in next to the dad, who was about an inch taller.

Thirty seconds later, he was on the second level and

assailant number two was none the wiser as to his whereabouts. But, until Ricky's man moved away from the concession stand, there wasn't really anything that Jimmy could do. It was far too public a spot to try to take him out. It would be better to focus his efforts on Marty.

While the boat was in motion, the parking area was restricted to working personnel only. Large signs every thirty feet warned that passengers were not allowed back on the parking deck. But the threat of a fine and rather flimsy metal chain across the entrance didn't offer much of an obstacle.

Jimmy waited until the nearest orange-vested worker turned his head and ducked through the entryway. Before stepping onto the parking deck, Jimmy flattened his body against the side paneling and once again surveyed the space.

It looked like Marty had almost finished on the lower deck. He strolled along the last row of vehicles, whistling a vaguely familiar tune as he finished his inspection.

This was Jimmy's cue to take action.

First, he checked to make sure there were no other workers in the nearby vicinity. Then he jogged down the first line of cars, in the opposite direction that Marty was moving. There were four rows altogether, each about fifteen cars deep. Once he reached the end of the row, he sprinted toward the next. The cars were parked closely together, almost bumper to bumper. When he was just one vehicle away from the end of the row, he paused and peeked between them. Sure enough, Marty was on the other side, peering into the rear window of a light blue minivan.

Utilizing the element of surprise, Jimmy vaulted forward, his arms outstretched to make contact with Marty. Unlike the larger thug in the bathroom who had seen his approach, Marty was caught completely unaware. He let out a yelp of surprise as he pitched face-first onto the cement flooring. Jimmy now had the upper hand by pressing his knee into his opponent's back while covering his mouth to muffle his screams.

Visibly stunned, Marty didn't seem inclined to continue the fight, offering only token resistance. Jimmy pulled out the gun he had seized earlier and pressed it against Marty's side.

"Now, you're going to do exactly as I say."

The dark head nodded.

"I'm going to take my hand off your mouth, but you better not make any noise." He waited for another nod. "Now tell me where I can get some rope."

Marty pointed to a yellow container about twenty feet away along the side of the boat.

"Walk with me." Jimmy pulled Marty up and marched him toward the container, all the while scanning to make sure that he hadn't been spotted. They were more in the open here than among the cars, but the ferry seemed to operate with a minimal number of workers, which allowed them to remain undetected by the rest of the staff. Still holding the pistol, Jimmy crouched down and then flung open the lid of the trunk. Sure enough, there was a spool of yellow acrylic rope inside. Setting down the gun, Jimmy wound the cord around Marty's wrists, knotting and re-knotting.

Next, he had to figure out where to stash Marty until they arrived at the port. Obviously, he wasn't going to shoot him. But he needed to ensure that he was out of commission until the ferry docked and he and Isobel made their escape.

The wind was beginning to pick up and his fingers were

growing numb. Without his sweatshirt, the October sunshine offered little warmth against the chilly temperatures.

Thud! What the—

The air was suddenly knocked out of him as someone ran full-force into his chest.

Henchman number three. Tall, blond and leering.

Now on the ground, Jimmy rolled to the left as a meaty fist flashed toward his face. The punch missed, and above him, he could hear curses as his assailant's hand made contact with the cement floor. With the blond man temporarily disabled, Jimmy ought to have had an edge. But pain suddenly ricocheted through his own body as a booted foot began to kick his side—Marty, his arms still bound tightly around his back, lashing out in the only way he could.

Jimmy responded in kind, kicking back against his blond attacker, knocking him off his feet. He wrapped his arms around his unbound opponent, now on the ground, and they both tried to prevail in the fight for survival. Their bodies rolled along the deck's hard floor.

He twisted his body again, trying to create some space between himself and the other man, but his blond assailant clung on. Blood pounded through his veins, and adrenaline coursed through his body.

And then he was tumbling.

Down. Down.

In his surprise, Jimmy released his grip on the other man's arm as realization suddenly dawned. They had fallen off the boat.

Half a second later, his body made impact with the cold water below.

Isobel peeked through the window of the first-aid office, hoping to catch a glimpse of Jimmy. The young woman who had introduced herself as Lucy had disappeared into the back closet, but the walkie-talkies on the cabinet suddenly crackled to life.

"We need assistance at the third level women's bathroom. Medical assistance at the bathroom needed."

A thread of fear began to wind its way down her spine. Was it Jimmy who was injured in a fight with one of Ricky's men? Should she call out to Lucy to let her know she was needed on deck?

Briinnnng! Briiinnnng! A small phone on the wall began to ring. "Hello?" Lucy was suddenly back in the room and had the receiver pressed to her ear. "What?...Uh-huh...Uh-huh. Okay. I'm coming now."

"Is someone hurt?" Isobel asked as soon as Lucy had set the phone down. The other girl made a wry expression.

"Someone found a man tied up in the women's bathroom. He's unconscious, so we'll probably need to bring him up here. Do you mind giving up the cot?"

Isobel was already scrambling upright. "No, no, not at all. I'm actually feeling better. But can I hold on to the jacket for a bit longer?"

"Huh?" Lucy was distracted as she pulled out her fanny pack and grabbed a few ice packs and a bottle of water. "Yeah, sure. I've got to go."

Isobel waited for the young woman to exit the small room and then she stood up, poised to follow. Yet the question still pricked at her brain. Who was the unconscious man? Didn't she need to find out? Indecision stilled her movements. But only for the span of a heartbeat.

Pulling the hood of the red jacket up over her head, Isobel slipped out of the first-aid station and joined the bystanders crowding outside the bathroom. Her heart thudded as the seconds seemed to tick by in slow motion. Finally, the door opened and Lucy and another attendant walked out carrying a backboard with a man strapped onto it.

Isobel glanced at the man's face and relief bloomed across her chest. It wasn't Jimmy. But she recognized the injured person as one of Ricky's men. So, Jimmy had managed to take at least one of their three pursuers out. Who knew where the other two were? Or Jimmy.

Isobel tapped her fingers against her leg. What to do next? Jimmy had advised her to stay hidden or to attempt to blend in with another group. Would it be too much of a risk to go back down to the second level and look around? The ferry ride was nearing the end of its journey. A flat strip of land was already visible on the east side of the lake. So maybe she should remain in place, hidden in the crowd, and wait for Jimmy's return.

She walked over to the guardrail and took three deep breaths. Then three more. She needed to remain calm, even in the event of adversity. Without even realizing what she was doing, her eyes began to scan the decks below her. With the wind picking up, there were more people huddled on the second deck. But there was no sign of Jimmy among them. She cast her eyes toward the cars. The Camaro was parked just as before. Second from the front, in the middle row.

The crew was preparing for their arrival at a frantic pace. Everyone seemed to be busy, hustling this way and that. Everyone except one person. She fixed her gaze on that solitary, stationary worker who was looking over the side of the boat. His arms tucked behind his back, he was holding a loop of bright yellow rope.

A tall, burlier man walked up to him. They chatted for a few minutes then both men turned away from the water. Horror washed over Isobel, and she could feel all her hairs along her neck and arms stand on edge as she realized she had been staring at a back view of Ricky's cousin. A cold shiver ran down her spine as she realized what that meant. So, Jimmy hadn't managed to take him out. Or had Marty taken out Jimmy? There had been something ominous in Marty's focus on the water.

She blinked back tears. She couldn't break down and cry. Not now. The wind suddenly seemed harsh and bitter, and the earlier sunshine had given way to darker clouds. Her fingers felt cold, so she tucked them inside the wind-breaker. But it didn't help. It was almost as if her heart and spirit had frozen on the inside.

Jesus, I need your help. Jimmy needs your help. Show us a way to make it off this boat.

The prayer provided some comfort. But, a moment later, the previously calm mood on the ferry began to shift to excitement.

"Ladies and gentleman," a voice blared from the speaker. "We are approaching Muskegon and will pull into port in five minutes. At that time, you can return to your vehicles and await directions to disembark. All tickets and IDs will be checked as you exit. We apologize for the delay."

Her ID would be checked again as she disembarked? Alice and Patrick hadn't mentioned that. Maybe it was just a formality. Or was this another tactic to find her?

The five-minute wait for the boat to pull along the dock and for the workers to secure it felt like an eternity. Isobel closed her eyes and concentrated her thoughts on Calvin, reliving all her best memories—the first time he rolled over, his giant, gummy smiles, his body cocooned in his sleep sack with only his round head peeking out.

Finally, there came an announcement that drivers should immediately return to their vehicles.

Jimmy's going to be there. He's going to be there, wait-

ing in the car, Isobel chanted in her head as she made her way down from the third deck to the Camaro. But no. The front seat was empty. She checked the back. Also empty.

Ignoring the sinking feeling in the pit of her stomach, Isobel climbed into the driver's seat. Her fingers tightened against the wheel, even though she wouldn't be pulling forward anytime soon. Her eyes scanned from left to right, looking for Jimmy and watching for Marty. Inside the glove compartment was a pair of aviator sunglasses, and she didn't waste any time putting them on and pulling the hood of her borrowed windbreaker even tighter against her head. Another long ten minutes and the car in front of her began to move forward at last.

Terror wrapped itself like a cloak around her body as a worker finally waved her car toward the ramp. Of course, it was Marty. And this time there was no place to hide. Keeping her head forward, she didn't even lower her gaze, but stared straight ahead into the cold, dark eyes of Ricky's cousin. He scowled, but motioned her forward. Thanks to the makeshift disguise, he hadn't recognized her.

But now she was off the boat and Jimmy still hadn't appeared. Slowly, the line of cars inched forward toward a small hut at the end of the dock.

"License and ticket, please," a voice ordered when she finally pulled up beside the ticketing window. She wanted to ask her if anything had happened to cause the delay. But she didn't dare. With trembling fingers, she pulled out her ticket and Alice's ID and handed them through the window. Would it work? She held her breath as the woman looked at her, then the ID, then back at her.

Then both were thrust back into her hands with the instruction to "Move along."

Okay. Moving along.

Somehow, she had made it off the ferry. Now she just needed to drive to a meeting place. She drove down the pier and turned out onto the main road that ran along the lakeshore. It only took five minutes to cover two miles from the spot where she had disembarked.

Whispering another prayer, she pulled off at a scenic overlook and then cast her eyes in both directions.

There was no sign of Jimmy.

TWELVE

The lake was cold. How cold, exactly, Jimmy couldn't say. Hadn't he read somewhere that a person could survive for about an hour in sixty-degree water, but only fifteen minutes in temperatures closer to fifty? That was kind of an important difference in determining whether or not someone would survive or perish.

His legs churned against the darkness below. Turning his face toward the sky, he did a quick calculation in his head. At this point, it had been at least a quarter of an hour since he'd fallen from the deck. Yet it seemed that no one had sent up an alarm about men overboard or spotted bodies in the lake. Maybe the pulsing roar of the engine had muffled any cries coming from the water as the ferry moved closer to the dock on the shore. Whatever the reason, it seemed that he was on his own.

The icy numbness permeating his limbs seemed to be easing a bit, which couldn't be a good sign considering that exhaustion had dimmed his other senses and was numbing his judgment. He was a reasonably good swimmer, but what had started as a sort of modified crawl stroke toward the shore had morphed into an extremely pathetic doggy paddle in an attempt to cover what was increasingly becoming an insurmountable distance to the shore.

If ever there was a time to find solace in prayer, this was it. He needed to believe that Isobel was still alive, that Ricky's men had not been able to discover her hiding place. But the real test would have come once they docked. Forcing his arms out of the water as he took another stroke, he pictured Isobel, still wearing that baggy red windbreaker, her eyes fixed and determined, looking exactly as she had when he'd left her on the ferry.

Please, God. Protect her.

He couldn't be sure that he had spoken the words out loud, but he had formed them in his heart.

He closed his eyes and imagined Isobel driving along the road by the lake, searching for a place to await his arrival. He hoped she wouldn't linger even one second longer than the twenty-minute limit they had agreed upon when they'd made their plan. He should have pushed back harder against the idea of a meeting place along the shore.

Of course, he hadn't expected to end up in the water. Worst-case scenario at that point involved them being separated on board the boat and then linking up a safe distance from the ferry. And twenty minutes was far too long for Isobel to wait. It was way too risky, especially since Ricky's men would likely have fanned out in their search. Why hadn't he insisted that she set off immediately for Detroit?

Because he wasn't going to make it; he knew that now. Not in twenty minutes. Not if he had all the time in the world. Though he was low in the water, he could still see a blurry outline of the shore. By even a generous estimate, it had to be at least a mile from where he was in the water. There was no way he could cover even a tenth of that distance, given the leaden fatigue of his arms and legs.

He had never been a quitter, even when his parents died and his family had been broken. But this wasn't a lack of will or determination. This was cold, hard reality pressing home the fact that every ragged breath he took could be his last.

Regrets and misgivings tumbled through his brain. He thought back to the raid on the safe house, trying to understand why it happened when it did. Isobel had insisted that she didn't have any solid information linking Ricky to any specific crimes. So why the move to take her out if she was just a background witness in the trial?

Unless she knew more than she realized. There was always the possibility that Isobel had witnessed something significant that would be revealed at trial. But it was much more likely that pure vindictiveness and revenge was powering Ricky's vendetta against his ex-wife.

As a towering wave crashed down on his head, frustration once again gripped his senses. He needed to reclaim the insight that just a moment ago had seemed so clear. Somewhere in his memory lay a critical clue. How had he lost it?

Despite the cold and the fatigue, he struggled to regain some sense of clarity about being in the safe house the day before the raid. Who was in the room with Isobel that first day? Stephanie, of course. Len and Meredith, too. He remembered that the two marshals had both hung around for a while after their shift. Ryan was there, too, bouncing around, playing with Calvin and doing push-ups on the living room floor.

It was all so clear, but then memory faded as he found himself slowly slipping under the black water. He was so cold. And so tired. It would almost be a relief to stop fighting, to stop thinking and give in to the inevitable sooner rather than later. What did any of it matter anyway? He wasn't going to make it. It was time to surrender to the deep drowsiness invading his senses. But even as he began to relax, his conscious nature rebelled against it. He couldn't stop fighting. There was too much at stake for that.

As he bobbed to the surface and opened his mouth to pull in another desperate lungful of air, his brain registered a discordant sound—the puttering of a motor and then, a moment later, a voice calling out across the water. He forced himself to attempt another stroke when strong arms reached down and grabbed him under his shoulders, pulling him up, out of the water. One final yank and he slid like a caught fish into the rough bottom of a small wooden boat.

"Not a great day for a swim," a gruff voice bellowed close to his ear.

He opened his mouth to speak, wanting to say something clever in response. But no sound came out. Just uncontrollable coughing as he struggled for air.

"Take your time, son," the man piloting the small craft advised. "Here. Take this." His rescuer tossed an old tartan blanket toward him.

Shivering, Jimmy wrapped it around his shoulders, grateful for the warmth. He stared at the grizzled face of the man sitting next to the outboard motor.

"Thank you. You saved my life." His voice sounded slurred and unrecognizable.

"No need for that. I was sitting here fishing when I saw something bobbing in the water. Thought it was a piece of debris washing in to the shore. Turned out to be you." The man chuckled and then stuck out his hand. "Zack Keith. Christian. Fisherman. And Green Bay Packers fan."

"I'm…" Jimmy struggled to form his words. "Jimmy. Jimmy Flynn."

"Well, nice to meet you, Mr. Flynn. Even in these particular circumstances. I'm going to guess that you fell off the ferry. Am I right?"

Jimmy nodded. It hurt to move his head. "Can...you... take me to shore?"

He was spouting gibberish—at least that was how it sounded to his ears. But his rescuer seemed to understand.

"I'd rather take you to a hospital," the man said.

Jimmy shook his head. His tongue seemed all tangled in his mouth, making it impossible to explain why that wasn't an option.

"Please, no," was all he managed to say.

The older man—Zack Keith—frowned and rubbed his chin as he seemed to mull over the issue. He must have made a decision because he shifted his grip on the throttle, increased his speed and pointed the bow of his boat toward the shore.

"I'm meeting someone," Jimmy choked out. But was that even true? Less than ten minutes earlier, he had decided that if Isobel had any sense, she would have given up on waiting and headed for Detroit. But something— some weird kind of feeling deep in his heart—made him understand that, despite the danger and the uncertainty of the situation, she would not leave Muskegon without him. "Red windbreaker," he said, surprised by his ability to even remember such a fact.

"And where is this meeting supposed to take place? This here's a pretty big body of water."

"North," Jimmy said. "Two miles from the landing."

Zach leaned forward and squinted toward the shore-line. "I suppose I could do that. Hang on. It's bound to get choppy closer to shore."

Jimmy closed his eyes, exhausted by the demands of the

conversation and secure in the knowledge that what happened next was now out of his control.

The sun emerged from the clouds to ride low in the sky, its light adding a dim sparkle to the gray waters of the lake.

Forty-five minutes down and counting.

A trickle of fear began to soak though Isobel's senses as she checked the clock on the Camaro's console. Another minute had passed in the countdown since she had pulled into a spot in the car park facing the road.

Where was Jimmy? None of the options were great as she considered the likely reasons to explain his delay.

He could still be on the ferry, receiving medical attention after being injured in a fight with Marty or one of the others. That wouldn't be the worst, considering the other alternative—that he had been waylaid onshore by a welcome party of Ricky's men.

Please, God. Let him be alive.

A sudden movement near the lakeshore caught her eye. She tented her eyes and peered toward an older man in tan overalls struggling to pull his rowboat onto beach. The man lifted his hand and wagged his fingers through the air.

Was he waving at her?

The man with the boat continued to motion in her direction. She glanced again to the left and to the right. No one else was around to heed his summons. She looked again at the man and this time he met and held her gaze. Did he know what had happened to Jimmy?

She'd have to go down to the shore to find out.

But she would need to cross the two-lane motorway to get to the beach, and that would be a risk. The men who had been looking for her could be anywhere, and she'd be a target the moment she stepped onto the road.

The man's wild gestures became more insistent as he pointed downward to something in his boat. The glare of the slowly setting sun cast the scene into shadows, making it hard for her to see what he was trying to show her. She slipped on her sunglasses and took a closer look.

It was a body. Jimmy's body.

A gasp escaped her throat.

She took off at a sprint and reached the shore in minutes, her heart seeming to double its frantic beat at the sight of Jimmy lying unconscious on the bottom of the boat.

"Is he alive?" she asked, her voice shaking.

"Near enough. I checked his pulse and it was okay. But he'd have been in the water for quite a while if he fell off the ferry. I'm no doctor, but I'd say he has a concussion. I told him that he needs to get himself checked out by medical professionals, but he paid no heed to that. But you're calling the shots now. I have my cell if you want to call an ambulance."

Jimmy provided the answer by lifting his head and raising his voice to a raspy croak. "No doctor."

Isobel looked at the older man and shrugged. "I'll figure out what to do once I get him into the car. But I might need help lifting him into the back seat."

The man nodded. "If your vehicle is nearby, it might be easier if you drove down and parked on the shoulder."

"Okay." She turned and sprinted back across the road. Her hands were shaking as she pushed the key in the ignition, but the motor started right up. Moments later, she pulled into a spot along the road.

Jimmy's whole body seemed to be shaking as she slung an arm around his waist and stepped sideways to allow the fisherman to hoist him up by the shoulders. Supported on either side, he was able to maintain an upright position long enough to stagger to the Camaro. Cars whizzed by as Isobel used her free hand to open the car door and, through careful maneuvering, helped get Jimmy situated in the back seat.

Isobel slipped off her windbreaker and draped it across Jimmy's chest. It wouldn't add much warmth, but it was better than nothing. For the first time since they had been together on the boat, Isobel got a good look at him. There was a wide gash across his forehead. His soaked clothing was caked with mud and grime.

The older man's gaze tracked from Jimmy to Isobel.

"Listen, miss. I don't know what's going on here. But I've spent seventy-two years so far on God's green earth, and I've got a pretty good record for knowing the good ones from the bad. And this young man of yours…" He gazed down at Jimmy and shook his head. "Well, he looks like one of the good guys."

Isobel swallowed the lump that had been forming in her throat. She didn't need to be convinced about Jimmy's integrity and courage. It touched her heart that this stranger recognized it, too.

"Thank you," she said, forcing a smile.

"You're welcome," he replied. "I wasn't going to mention it, but I was listening to the radio. And there's some sort of alert being issued about a couple of men who disappeared from the ferry. Not much more information than that. Just that both were wanted for questioning about an assault on the ship. Now, I tend to be skeptical about most of what I hear on the news, so you can put that in your back pocket and decide what to do with it."

A jolt of fear shot up from Isobel's spine. The last thing they needed was to involve the police. It would help if she knew what had actually happened on the boat, but there'd be time enough to hear the whole story from Jimmy once he recovered. For now, she could only be grateful for the kindness of strangers.

"You saved his life," she said.

The man turned and lumbered back to his boat, raising his hand as if to say *no problem*. She twisted the key in the ignition and waited for a break in the traffic before she turned onto the road. She knew from looking at the map Patrick had left in the glove compartment that, if she stayed the course, they could pick up I-96, which would take them to Detroit.

But she wasn't sure that was where they needed to go.

From the back seat came a groan.

Could Jimmy sense her hesitation? Because heading east didn't seem like a clear call. Jimmy was clearly suffering from hypothermia after so much time in the water. And most likely a concussion, given his inability to focus for more than a few seconds at a time.

And going to the hospital could mean involving the police, who might make the connection to the assault on the ferry.

It wouldn't bode well for Jimmy to be put in jail. Not here. Not now.

Jimmy hadn't said much, but he had made it clear he didn't want to go to the hospital. And from the little she knew about concussions and hypothermia, it would be foolhardy to subject someone with Jimmy's injuries to a six-and-a-half-hour journey in the back seat of a car.

He needed dry, warm clothes. A quiet place to rest. Food and water. And time to recover from his injuries.

They wouldn't be going to the hospital. Nor would they be heading for Detroit.

There was one more option she hadn't considered.

She flicked on her turn signal and prepared to turn around at the next intersection.

THIRTEEN

Ludington, Michigan, was a straight shot up US-31. Though tempted to put pedal to the metal to save on time, Isobel stuck to the speed limit, so it was just after six thirty when she pulled up to the Cullen cottage on Giles Drive.

Jimmy had slept the whole way, despite her nonstop chatter aimed at keeping him awake. Hadn't she read somewhere that it was critical for a person suffering from a concussion to refrain from sleeping for at least five hours after the injury? But at this point, there was nothing she could do about that.

Patrick's note in hand, she headed up the pathway through a wrought-iron gate askew on its hinges. When she reached the front door, she tapped in the code. The mechanism clicked, and with a gentle push, the door swung open.

From the look of the landscaping, she had been expecting the inside of the cottage to be nice, but it was even nicer than she had hoped for, cozy and comfortable but not at all fussy. She found the thermostat and turned the heat up to seventy. Then she grabbed a couple of flannel sheets to cover the sofa as well as some pillows and a throw from a wicker basket by the door and made a cozy spot for Jimmy to rest.

Back at the car, she did her best to rouse Jimmy. It would

be impossible to get him out of the car without his cooperation.

"Up at and 'em, Marshal Flynn," she said, snaking her arm around his waist and pulling him upright. "We've reached our destination, and our top priority at the moment is getting you inside."

Then, it was one slow step at a time as they hobbled, like two kids in a three-legged race, toward the house. Isobel kept her eyes on the path, scanning for anything that might cause a stumble and hoping none of the neighbors were watching and wondering about two strangers making themselves at home in the house next door.

Once they reached the living room, she allowed Jimmy to collapse on the couch. She had planned for it to be a temporary stop, but Jimmy closed his eyes and leaned back against the pillows.

"I guess you can wait on a shower. But at least let me help you change out of those wet clothes."

Jimmy's eyes blinked open as the realization of what she was suggesting dawned. With difficulty, he pushed himself up on his elbow, wavering a bit as he choked out his reply. "I'll do it myself."

Progress. A full sentence, though mostly slurred.

She fished through the items Patrick had lent them for their journey, pulling out a pair of sweatpants, a soft tee shirt and a fleece top, and set them next to Jimmy on the couch.

"I'm going to see if I can find the Cullens' medical stash. I'd like to put some disinfectant on that cut. And a couple of Tylenol will go a long way toward taking the edge off when the pain kicks in later tonight."

It didn't take long for her to find what she was looking for on the top shelf of a bedroom closet. She filled a glass of water from the kitchen tap then headed back to the living room and knelt beside Jimmy, where she soaked a cotton ball with disinfectant and dabbed it on the gash on his forehead.

"Might sting a bit," she said. She helped him pull himself into a sitting position and handed him two tablets of Tylenol, holding the glass so he could wash down the meds.

"Thanks, Isobel." Jimmy smiled and touched her hand. The gesture was so sweet and trusting that her heart exploded with gratitude. She owed this man her life. And so much more.

Uh-oh. She pulled in a deep breath. She had to be careful here. The last thing she needed was to make the classic mistake of falling hard for her rescuer. That couldn't happen now, not ever, given all the issues already on her plate.

She stood up quickly and put on her game face. Stern caregiver, taking charge of the patient. The last thing she needed was to give in to the emotional tug pulling at her heart.

"While you get out of those wet clothes, I'll rustle up dinner."

She headed into the kitchen, but soon discovered "rustling up" something delicious and warm for dinner would prove to be a challenge. After opening and closing a half dozen cabinets, all she had found that was edible was an unopened box of Lorna Doone cookies. When she had more time, she'd explore the freezer and the drawers next to the sink.

She put the kettle on the stovetop and boiled some water, which she poured over the teabags she had placed in the mugs. She added the cookies to the tray and carried it into the living room.

Jimmy was sitting up, dressed in dry sweatpants and a tee. He appeared extremely pleased with this accomplishment.

"Well done, you," she said, hiding her smile as she gathered up the wet clothes that had been tossed on the floor. "Want some help with that sweatshirt?"

He shook his head. "Car in the garage," he said.

Right. Leave it to Jimmy to make sure they stayed under the radar by not advertising their presence by leaving the Camaro parked in the driveway.

She grabbed the keys and made her way out the door. By the time she returned, Jimmy had once again fallen asleep. She looked at the untouched cookies and mugs of tea on the tray and shrugged. He needed to eat, but sleep seemed more important at the moment.

Teatime for one then. But first, another trip to the kitchen to get the sugar. On the way out the door, she noticed the internet code on the bulletin board. FOX 34. She jotted it down on a scrap of paper and headed back to the living room to fire up the internet. She needed to learn all she could about concussions. And after that, she'd check out the information on the thumb drive about the trial.

Concussion symptoms: headache—check, slurred speech—check, fatigue—check. As far as she knew, the rest—including nausea, vomiting, amnesia and blurred vision—were so far not an issue.

The treatment was relatively simple. Take it easy and avoid screens and stress. "A quiet couple of days of rest can be quite a challenge for some people," the author of the online article about concussions claimed. "Especially children who often find it difficult to sit still."

She thought about Calvin, who had always been squirmy, even as an infant. Now that she was a parent, she had found herself interested in so many aspects of child development, even things she had never cared about before. Like the responsibility for teaching and leading by example. That would a challenge. As a single parent, she'd have to figure out most things all by herself.

Jimmy would make a good father when the time came for that. His actions were measured, and he was straightforward and honest, though far too tightlipped when it came to discussing his personal life. It amazed her how little she knew about his past, especially considering how much he knew about hers. They hadn't talked much when they were back at the safe house. She had usually gravitated to Ryan as a companion for dinner or watching TV. Of course, back then, she hadn't yet become aware of the finer points of Jimmy Flynn. Not only was he funny and interesting and competent in all ways, but he was also the perfect companion to have by her side in a crisis.

Her mind tracked back to Alice's reference to the mysterious Kim. There definitely was a story there, but it would be Jimmy's to tell when the time was right. But when would that be? Once Jimmy recovered, they would be on the way to Detroit where they would be surrounded by people asking questions and pulling them apart. It would be a relief to be safe, but she would miss the time she and Jimmy had spent together, the closeness and the friendship they had shared. Would he miss it too? Or was protecting her just part of his job?

She must have been staring, because when Jimmy opened his eyes, he gave her a strange look and she felt that she had been caught out. Did he realize she had been surreptitiously reviewing his many good traits in her head? A blush of heat spread across her cheeks and she felt suddenly sheepish.

"What?" he asked, pushing himself up on his elbows.

"Nothing." She shrugged. "I was just sitting here wondering if I should wake you up and try to get you to eat."

"I still feel kind of queasy."

She nodded. "I was just reading about concussions. Nausea is normal. So is temporary amnesia. Do you remember how you ended up in the lake?"

"A bit. I got blindsided by that huge friend of Marty's on the parking deck, and we went over the side together. I don't know what happened to him. One minute, he was treading water beside me. Then I turned my head and he had disappeared."

"And you got rescued by that fisherman?"

"Zach, I think his name was. Yeah. Zach. But that didn't happen right away. I was in the lake awhile before he pulled me out."

Isobel grimaced. "If I had known you were in trouble, maybe I could have helped."

"No. You did exactly what you were supposed to do. You stayed hidden and got off the ferry without getting caught, which was an amazing accomplishment." His lips bent into a wide smile. "I should have known you wouldn't leave town without me."

"Yeah, well." She blushed again. She needed to stop this. She was acting like a goofy teenager crushing on the quarterback of the high school team. "Once I checked out concussions, I was planning to look at the stuff on the thumb drive and give it a quick run-through."

"While you do that, I think I might be finally ready to take that shower you've been promoting."

"Good idea. But watch out for the faucets in the sink. The water tends to spray out of the basin."

"You know what? I just remembered what I was thinking about when I was trying to stay afloat in the lake."

"About the trial?"

"Yeah. I had this idea about the evening before the attack. It made sense then, but now?" He closed his eyes and pulled in a deep breath. "Not so much."

For the second time in two days, Jimmy awoke to the aroma of coffee wafting through the room. What time was it anyway? And why did every bone in his body ache? It felt like he had been mauled by King Kong.

Isobel must have heard him stirring, because she immediately stuck her head through the kitchen door. "Hey there, sleepyhead. How are you feeling this morning? Still a bit woozy? How about a couple of Tylenol before breakfast?"

"Yes, please." He pulled himself up with a minimum amount of groaning. "Not to worry. I'm much improved since yesterday. I actually think my appetite is back."

"Excellent." Isobel disappeared through the doorway and, a moment later, she shuffled back into the room with a full tray.

"Are those pancakes I see on that plate?"

"Yes, sir." Isobel set the tray on the table next to the couch and handed him two tablets of pain medicine and a mug of steaming coffee. "Courtesy of the Cullens' freezer. I don't know how we are going to repay them when this is over. Especially me, when I consider that they agreed to care for Calvin. I wonder how he's coping in a house full of kids."

"I'm sure he's fine," Jimmy assured her. All of a sudden, he was ravenously hungry and he dug into the breakfast with gusto as Isobel sipped her tea.

Five minutes later, he set down his fork and turned his gaze back to Isobel, who obviously had something important to say.

She leaned forward and cradled her chin in her hands. "Are you up for a serious conversation?"

"Sure." His eyes slid sideways, not certain where she was going with the question.

"Good. Because I was thinking that maybe we could stay here for a while and forget the trial. Think about it, Jimmy. What's the point of us rushing to get to Detroit? Even Stephanie admitted that my testimony would hardly be key toward getting a conviction. Ricky was always careful not to talk business when I was in the room. Sure, I began to notice that the things he told me didn't add up. And sure, I knew he was ruthless and temperamental. But as for concrete evidence…" She shrugged. "I was pretty much in the dark when it came to that stuff."

Jimmy took a deep breath. "Isobel, I…"

She was quick to interrupt. "Of course, we'd need to pick up Calvin from the Cullens'. But once he's with us, we can settle in and stay off the grid. I'd be more than good with that."

He would be, too, but he wasn't going to admit it. Being here, alone with Isobel, he felt lighter and more positive about life. But, as enticing as it was to think about staying, they didn't really have a choice. He had a job to do, and they both needed to finish what they had started. And that could only be accomplished in a Detroit courtroom.

To what end, though? Isobel claimed that she had no insider knowledge of Ricky Bashir's criminal enterprise. So calling her to the stand was unlikely to make any difference in the outcome of the trial. And given what Patrick had deduced after reading the articles on the thumb drive, the prosecution seemed to have an extremely weak case.

Isobel cleared her throat. "Um, Jimmy. Is everything okay? You look like you're a hundred miles away."

More like two hundred and fifty miles, watching Isobel face off with a defiant Ricky Bashir. But why add a pessimistic spin to what could well be their last morning together? Best to remain upbeat and optimistic.

"Nah. I was just thinking about how grateful I am that Patrick gave us the keys to this place. I was in rough shape yesterday. I don't know what we would have done if we hadn't been able to stay here last night. I feel so much better now. In fact, as soon as I take a shower and get dressed, we can get this show back on the road."

"As your temporary caregiver, I wouldn't recommend going anywhere until at least until twenty-four hours have passed since the concussion."

"It isn't necessary to follow the usual protocol. I'm feeling on top of the world at the moment."

"Let's see how you're doing after lunch." She laughed. "I like hearing all those old-school expressions you use. 'Top of the world. Get this show on the road.'"

"Hey." He pretended to be offended. "My dad used to say things like that all the time. I guess quite a few got imprinted on my brain."

Isobel's face turned serious. "Oh, Jimmy. Alice told me how they died in a car crash and how you took care of your younger siblings."

"'Took care of' is an inflated way of describing what I did. It was just the basics. They were all old enough to pitch in. And we had lots of help from neighbors and friends. In that first year after the accident, it felt like the loaves and fishes in that Bible story. I'd take a casserole out of the freezer, and two more would appear in its place."

"What about Kim? Was she able to help as well?"

Kim? How did Isobel know about Kim? But even as he asked the question, he knew the answer. "I'm guessing you heard that name from one Alice Cullen. But Kim doesn't figure in the story of what happened with my folks. She's more of a footnote to be discussed later."

Isobel nodded. She seemed to understand that she had overstepped the boundaries. "I get it. For a long time, I felt really guarded talking about Ricky. I never told anyone this before but I was so desperate to get away from him that I took the two hundred dollars I had stashed in my cosmetic case and left behind all of my jewelry and keepsakes from my past life. I did manage to grab one other thing which ties in to what you just said about the loaves and fishes." She walked across the room and picked up the bag Alice had lent her and pulled out a worn leather Bible.

"I carried this on the bus from Detroit, through Wisconsin and Minnesota. It has been a good and faithful friend along the way, something I could turn to during times of anxiety and fear. When we left the safe house, it was in the bag with Calvin's things, so it's been with us through these past few days—in the deer blind, at the hotel and even on the ferry. I can tell you a little more about how it's helped me if you're interested."

FOURTEEN

Talk about Jesus or discuss his relationship with Kim?

Jimmy settled back against the couch and tried to decide which subject would cause him the most angst.

He had downplayed Kim when Isobel had mentioned it earlier because it dredged up too many painful memories. Like he'd said before, it was a long story. Just because he had come to terms with what had happened didn't mean that he was ready to talk about it… And yet, he found himself wanting to tell her about it. She was a kind and caring person, and she'd been vulnerable with him when she'd spoken about Ricky. Maybe he could reveal his past to her.

Jimmy pulled in a long breath, suddenly aware that they seemed to have taken on new roles, Isobel as the therapist and him as the patient. And like a good psychologist, she had zoomed right in to the heart of the issue.

"Kim was my high school girlfriend," he began tentatively, not able to meet her gaze. "But even back then, we wanted different things in life. We were just so young that we didn't realize it. And when my parents died, it wasn't the right time to discuss the reasons why our relationship wasn't working. And our problems as a couple were easy to ignore since we were both so busy. She was going to school, getting her doctorate in early childhood education.

And I was trying to keep things together with my family and studying and working part-time. So, rather than break up, we got engaged."

Isobel raised her brow.

He laughed. "Made no sense, I know. But lots of our friends were taking the plunge, so we thought, Why not us? But then, at the rehearsal before the wedding, Kim pulled me aside and said she couldn't go through with it. I was blindsided, but apparently, I was the only one who hadn't seen the signs. And then it turned out that she had already started dating my brother."

Her face went slack with surprise. "Your brother? Isn't he…?"

"Yeah. He's seven years younger. Crazy, right? I lost my girlfriend, my little brother and my self-respect in one fell swoop." He'd tried say it lightly, but even after all these years, the betrayal still stung.

Isobel's countenance revealed her dismay. "That must have been awful."

"For a while, it was. I tried to act like I didn't have a problem with them being together. That didn't work, so I left town and joined the marshals. Learned a few skills. Met you. So, quite a few good things came of it, too."

Her eyes widened in surprise. Had he said too much? Maybe he shouldn't be telling her all this. But she smiled and reached for his hand, sending his heart skittering. "I'm glad we met, too. What's your brother's name?"

"Lucas." He swallowed hard. "Luke, for short."

Isobel squeezed his hand. He was hoping they could stay like that, with their fingers entwined, for the rest of the day. But after a few minutes, she let go.

"Thanks for opening up to me about all of this for telling

me about Luke and Kim and your decision to move away from your hometown. It must have been tough."

"It was, but it was freeing, too. I had to leave. Otherwise, I'd stay stuck in a hard place by humiliation and obligation. Much later, when I was able get some distance from what had happened and to analyze my motives, I realized that I was following the same template I had when my parents died, keeping my head down and pretending everything was okay. But that got harder and harder as time went on."

He'd never told anyone about any of this before, had never even formed the words in his heart. Why was Isobel so easy to talk to? Maybe because he knew she'd faced her share of struggles. Or maybe because she was the first person he had trusted for a long time.

"I know that leaving home was a good decision. I was hanging on by a thread, and every week brought some new challenge. Seeing Luke and Kim together at my sister's apartment. Visiting the happy couple at Christmas. Hearing that they had tied the knot in Vegas. Attending a housewarming party when they bought their first place." He shook his head. "One moment in particular made me realize that I had to stop being this fake person who was always smiling and acting glad. It was when Kim announced that they were expecting their first kid. My brother walked up to me, anticipating a high five. I raised my hand in the air and then stopped. Held it there as if it were frozen. I suddenly thought, What am I doing? Of course, part of me was glad that Luke was going to be a dad. But why was it always on me to act like everything was okay? Because it didn't feel okay. It felt humiliating. I knew then that it was time for a change. I moved to Detroit, and you pretty much know the rest of the story."

Isobel smiled. "You decided to work toward your own happy ending."

He nodded. The embarrassment and humiliation had dissipated, and he'd moved on. And though he didn't harbor any more feelings for Kim, he regretted that the breakup had led to losing his brother.

Come to think of it, discussing Jesus might be an easier conversation all around.

Isobel still clutched her Bible to her chest, her eyes shining with understanding. Oh, well. Why not? They weren't going anywhere, at least until after lunch.

He took a deep breath, gesturing at her Bible.

"I'd like to hear more about how God's word became such a comfort to you since I've been fairly resistant to all that stuff. My folks took me to church when I was a kid, but all that 'Jesus saves' preaching never stuck. I had already started to drift away from organized religion when my parents were in the accident. And once they died, I really couldn't find a place for God in the equation. I focused all my energy on doing what I had to do to make it through each day, and reading the Bible and going to church were just distractions. I knew my parents would have wanted me to do better for my sake as well as my siblings', but I just didn't have the energy." He took a deep breath, wondering if the conversation had taken a turn into more challenging territory. "You get that, don't you? You must have felt the same sense of being alone and desperate when you were married to Ricky."

Isobel nodded. "I did. There were days when the only thing I could think about was staying out of his way. Not that he hit me, or anything like that. He was just so cold and cruel in his disapproval. And it seemed like everything

I did disappointed him. The way I dressed. The things I talked about when we'd meet his friends for dinner. I didn't have any close confidantes. Ricky made sure of that. But then I opened the Bible and started to read. It was tough going at first, since there was so much there that I didn't understand. But there was a lot that gave me hope and inspiration. Later, when I moved to Dagger Lake, I joined a group who were studying Mark's gospel, and that got me to dig deeper. If you'd like, I could show you some of my favorite verses. Maybe something would click that would help you, too."

"I'd like that at some point. In fact, you'd be pleased to hear that I actually prayed yesterday for the first time in years. It was when I was in the water and I was sure I was going to drown."

"You asked God to save you?" Isobel wanted to know.

"Yeah," he lied. What would she think if he told the truth—that even as he was certain he was taking his last breath, his prayer to God was for her? He forced a smile. "This is a conversation we should definitely have somewhere down the line."

Isobel shot him a look of skepticism. "Somewhere down the line?"

"I mean it. I'd like to hear more about your faith journey, and maybe get some tips for reading the Bible a bit on my own. But right now, I think we need to check out the stuff I loaded on the thumb drive. It could have some relevance to your testimony."

"Haven't you already gone through most of that with Patrick?"

"I did. But there were a couple things we didn't get to."

Isobel set her Bible down and opened the computer. "Okay. I'll pull it up. Remember, though—you're recovering from a concussion. You aren't supposed to be staring at screens."

Apparently, their religious discussion was over, at least for the moment. He was glad that reading the Bible helped Isobel deal with Ricky. And though he wasn't totally sold on the concept, at some point he might be willing to give it a try. Just not right now, when he needed to concentrate on preparing for the trial.

Isobel's fingers clicked against the keyboard, stopping on a series about the court case from the *Detroit Free Press*.

"See if you can find the article with pictures of some of your ex-husband's associates. Patrick and I gave it just a cursory glance, but it did look interesting."

Isobel continued to scroll, pausing when she came to a four-page spread titled "The Missing Friends of Ricky Bashir." She angled the screen so he could see the photographs of Ricky's associates who had disappeared under mysterious circumstances.

"Recognize anyone?" Jimmy asked.

"No. Not him," she said, scrolling past the first pictures at the top. "Definitely not him. Or him either." She paused on a small photo at the bottom of the page and widened the screen for a closer look. "Now, this guy I do know. His name is Sam Hunt. He used to stay at our place for the weekend sometimes. Nice guy." She paused to read the text. "It says here he's missing and presumed dead."

Jimmy found the continuation of the story on the next page. "There's a definite suggestion here that Sam Hunt was an undercover agent working for Homeland Security. If that's true, it's probably safe to assume that Ricky discovered what this guy was up to and took him out." Jimmy glanced at Isobel, whose eyes had filled with tears, and immediately regretted his blunt tone. "Sorry to put it like that. Especially since he was a good friend of yours."

Her bottom lip quivered. "I wouldn't say good friend, but definitely a friendly acquaintance. I really didn't spend enough time with him to make a real connection. But..." She trailed off, as if wrapped in a memory. "He was kind. Most of Ricky's associates were polite, probably because they were afraid of Ricky, but Sam seemed genuine. He used to ask me what I was reading and what kinds of fiction I liked best."

Jimmy's gut told him there was more to the story than just friendly curiosity. "Did any of this come up during trial prep at the safe house?"

Isobel thought for a minute. "It's hard to remember. During that first day with Stephanie, so much was discussed. Even Len and Meredith stuck around after their shifts had ended to hear the inside scoop of what marriage to a mob boss was really like."

"Did that bother you?"

She shrugged. "Sure, it did. It was really embarrassing. I liked everyone, and I wanted them to like me. I'm sure they were all thinking I was sort of a dope for taking so long to realize that the man I had married was a criminal. I didn't get mad, though. I knew the point was to prepare me for all the mudslinging by the defense when I took the stand."

Jimmy's lips bent in a sympathetic smile. "I recall feeling uncomfortable that you were being forced to relive such painful memories. But you were a rock star."

"Thanks, Jimmy."

"Of course. Is it possible that Ricky was jealous of your friendship and had him killed in a jealous rage?"

Isobel laughed. "No way. Ricky thought he was a nerd, always talking about literature to anyone who would listen. I'm sure his disappearance didn't have anything to do with me."

"I'm not trying to make you feel defensive. I've just been thinking back to what happened before the raid on the safe house. The timing of the attack is what's confusing me, the way it all went down so close to the time you were set to take the stand. Why? What was Ricky afraid of, since he had to know that you wouldn't be a key witness in the trial? I keep coming back to this connection to Sam Hunt. Did you tell him you were pregnant and planning to leave Ricky?"

Isobel's eyes flashed indignantly. "Of course not. I told you before. It wasn't like that between us." She was quiet for a moment, and then she blew out a long sigh. "I wish I had a better memory about everything that was said during the trial brief, but I'm coming up blank. It was a pretty intense process, but it did ease a bit in the evening after you and Ryan went off shift. Someone said something about the books we had brought along to the safe house. Meredith was ten pages into a nine-hundred-page novel about Benjamin Franklin, and she offered to lend it to me when she was finished. We all laughed about that. And then I said that I hadn't been able to curb my love of thrillers, despite having a friend who gave me a couple of challenging books and wouldn't accept any excuse about why I was too busy to read them. And then someone—Len, I think—asked what the titles were."

"The friend that gave you the books was Sam Hunt?"

She nodded.

"Did you mention his name?"

She shrugged. "Probably. I might have said that he was a friend of Ricky's."

"What books did he give you?"

Isobel shrugged. "*A Tale of Two Cities*. I didn't actually read it, but maybe someday. *To Kill a Mockingbird*. That one I did start, but I never got around to finishing it. And, of course, this." Isobel reached across the table and picked up her Bible. "This was the only one I did read. Not cover-to-cover. I skipped some parts. But it helped me understand God's plan for my salvation. I can truly say that it saved my life."

Jimmy leaned forward in his seat. "Do you mind if I look at your Bible?"

"Of course not." She handed him the leather-bound book, watching as he opened it to the page where a thin green ribbon held her place. The words she had been reading were etched in her heart. *Have mercy upon me, O God, according to thy lovingkindness: according unto the multitude of thy tender mercies blot out my transgressions.*

"I was reading the psalms when I woke up this morning." She watched as Jimmy continued to thumb through the pages. "What are you hoping to find?"

"I don't know." He shrugged. "A piece of paper, thin and small enough to be stuck between the pages. It's just a hunch, but maybe Sam Hunt realized that he had been made and he slipped his evidence into the Bible where he knew it would be safe."

"But I read it every day. Wouldn't I have found it by now?"

"Maybe. Or it could have fallen out at some point without you noticing. What about the other books he gave you?"

"I didn't take them when I left. I told Sam I probably wouldn't get around to reading them for a while, so I guess he could have seen that as a hint that I was planning to leave

Ricky. But the more I think about it, the more I'm sure that he wouldn't have used me that way. He wasn't like that."

"Maybe he was desperate. Maybe he saw you as his only possible ally who could help him bring down Ricky."

"Why would he think I'd be willing to betray my husband?"

"He probably recognized that you were a kind and caring person who would do the right thing when the time was right."

"Well, if he thought that, then I really did let him down." She made a fist with her fingers and shook her head. "I ran away and never looked back. Anyway, how could any of this be related to the raid on the safe house?"

"I don't know. I'm just grasping at straws here, trying to make sense of it."

Maybe so, but she couldn't help feeling that she wasn't the person that either Sam Hunt or Jimmy thought she might be. She had stumbled blindly into a marriage with a mob boss without realizing it. And then, even when she'd begun to suspect the enormity of Ricky's crimes, she had done nothing to expose the truth. Her only response was to run away and build a new life for herself and her baby, leaving everything and everyone behind. Even Sam Hunt.

She set down the computer and stretched her arms toward the ceiling. "I feel sick when I think about my mistakes. Poor Sam. If Ricky hurt him, it's one more thing that's on me."

"Don't be so hard on yourself, Isobel. You couldn't have realized what was going on—with Sam or with Ricky."

Did Jimmy really believe that? How could he after reading about the closet full of designer clothing and the lavish lifestyle described in her file?

"Still, I should have been a lot more aware of what was going on around me."

A shadow of recognition shaded Jimmy's countenance. Had he been in a similar place with someone he'd thought he loved?

She couldn't ask. He had made it clear that the subject of Kim was now off limits. She tilted her head toward the kitchen. "I don't know about you, but all this talk is making me thirsty. I could do with one more cup of tea before we continue our conversation."

As she moved across the room, she could see Jimmy reach across the table and claim the computer, his fingers racing nimbly across the keys.

"Hey. No screens. Remember?"

"What difference does it make if it's something you show me or something I pull up myself? It's a screen, no matter what."

Fair point. But her pleasant companion of just a few minutes ago seemed to have morphed into an irascible grouch. Was Jimmy mad at her because of what she had let happen to Sam Hunt? Or because his friends on the protective unit had died to protect someone who had turned out to be a poor friend and a pretty lame witness to boot? He'd been so open with her moments ago, talking about Kim. Now he seemed like a closed book. Did he regret telling her about his past?

She slipped out to the kitchen to fetch her tea.

But crabby Jimmy was still in residence when she returned, steaming mug in hand. He closed the computer, stood up and started tossing his clothes in a heap on the floor, even the ones she had washed, dried and set in a neat pile next to the couch.

"Time to hit the road," he said.

"Jimmy. Slow down. We still need to have lunch and…"

He shook his head. "I'll grab those cookies from the kitchen and we can eat them on the road. We need to go," Jimmy said.

"Sorry?" she said, not sounding sorry. "Why the sudden hurry?"

"I just went online to check in on the trial. The prosecution plans to wrap up today, and there's a chance the defense will rest as well."

Her chest tightened. So soon? "Doesn't Ricky's attorney plan to call any witnesses?"

"Apparently not. He must think that the prosecution didn't prove their case and that an acquittal is in the bag. But if we can get there while the trial is still in progress, maybe…" He let the possibility hang in the air.

"Maybe what? I told you, I don't have anything to say that will change the outcome of the case. Even if I did, it wouldn't matter because we'll never make it on time. Detroit is over six hours away. And that's assuming we don't hit traffic." Her chance to nail Ricky wasn't this trial, but when she testified about the bank robbery and child abduction out of state.

"We have to try," he said, snatching the car keys and heading for the front door.

Isobel could feel her heart racing as she reacted to the frantic energy bouncing off Jimmy. She didn't want to leave—she wanted the refuge of the cottage for just a bit longer—but she locked up and followed him to the car.

The first stretch of the drive passed in silence, Jimmy's dark eyes fixed resolutely on the road as she sat, her legs curled up under her in the passenger seat, lips pressed together in a tight frown. Maybe he was disappointed in her, but that was unfair. Sure, she had enjoyed the perks of being Ricky's wife, the unlimited spending and the maids and assistants to care for her needs. She had walked away from all that, hadn't she? And as for the rest, how could she possibly be expected to remember every single word she had spoken during the trial prep, let alone every interaction she'd had with Sam Hunt?

But there was no escaping the fact that agents who had risked their lives to protect her had ended up dead. Her shoulders felt heavy from the mantle of blame. She felt alone and bereft, lacking the comfort of her little boy. She wished Jimmy would talk to her. She'd loved hearing about his family and his life and the journey that had led him to carving out a new place and new life.

Two hours into their journey, she couldn't hold on to her silence any longer. "I don't understand what's going on. Why have we suddenly moved into this crazy, fast gear?"

He cut his eyes toward her. "Because we need to get you to Detroit to testify. That has always been the plan, though I seem to have forgotten it along the way. I let myself..." He paused and shook his head. "Think about it, Iz. Sam Hunt went undercover to get the goods on Ricky and ended up paying with his life. Compared to him, what have I been doing besides lounging on the sofa, eating pancakes and acting like I accomplished something great by dodging a few bad guys? If Ricky gets acquitted, he'll continue to act above the law, murdering Homeland Security agents, bombing banks and trying to kidnap his son. And the danger to you is never going to end."

"Stop it, Jimmy." Her voice shook with emotion as she struggled to refute what he had said. "First of all, you haven't been lazing around taking it easy. You almost drowned protecting me on the ferry. And you seem to have forgotten there'll be another trial in Dagger Lake. Even if

Ricky's found not guilty in Detroit, he will still face judgment in North Dakota. And no way will he be able to corrupt any witnesses there."

Jimmy fixed her with a stony glare. "That's the part I didn't want to mention. When you went to the kitchen for tea, I saw a news story online about the kidnapping, attempted murder and conspiracy charges in the case in Dagger Lake being dropped due to a Fourth Amendment technicality."

Isobel felt the air leave her lungs. "What? How?"

Jimmy shook his head. "At this point, it doesn't matter how. What's important is that this trial in Detroit could be our last chance to make sure your ex-husband stays in jail."

FIFTEEN

Traffic had been light on the journey east, and barring any unforeseen delays, they were on pace to arrive in Detroit by three in the afternoon. First stop would be the federal building, headquarters of the US Marshals and courthouse for the eastern district of Michigan. What happened next would be anyone's guess.

It was possible that Isobel would be immediately whisked off to the courtroom and called to the stand. That would be best-case scenario. For Jimmy, only one thing was absolutely certain, and that was that he would be expected to give an account of his whereabout for past four days, an explanation of what had gone down during the raid on the safe house and the reasons he had chosen to stay off the grid.

There were things Jimmy wanted to know as well. What had the recovery team found at the safe house? Had anyone survived the initial attack? Had Ryan recovered from his injuries? Was there any progress in identifying the mole?

Jimmy glanced at Isobel, who appeared to be asleep. Then again, maybe she was just pretending. He wouldn't blame her if she was. When she woke up, he'd apologize for the sharp tone of their previous conversation. He knew she hadn't wanted to leave the cottage in Ludington. Neither had he. And that was the problem in a nutshell, just like all the other missteps taken during their flight.

He was the one who'd suggested they stop at the Cullens' and then decided they should take the ferry to Michigan. He was the one who had slow walked their return to headquarters, reveling in his time with Isobel and the close bond they had formed as friends. His boss was definitely going to accuse him of going rogue, but the bottom line was that Isobel was safe. Though maybe not for long, without a marshal by her side.

For one crazy moment, Jimmy's thoughts raced ahead of him to a life as Isobel's full-time bodyguard. That was crazy since neither of them wanted that. She didn't, for sure. But as long as her ex was out there, the danger was not going away.

So, now what? Even if they made it to Detroit before the defense rested, there was a fair chance that it would be too late for any further witnesses to be called to the stand. And, as Isobel had been quick to point out, she really didn't have a lot to say. Her presence could only serve to inflame Ricky, particularly if she was asked to talk about her marriage.

He shook off the image of Ricky Bashir fuming in a front-row seat in the courtroom as a bump in the road startled Isobel awake. She opened her eyes and swiveled around to face him.

"Hi," he said.

"Right back atcha," she said, sounding more sleepy than mad.

Apology time.

"I'm sorry for how I acted before. I tend to let problems become magnified in my head."

She bent her lips upward in a sad sort of smile. "I get it. The whole point of your mission was to get me across the finish line so I could testify. And even if the prosecution failed to get a conviction, there was always the case in Dagger Lake. So, the idea of Ricky going free sends chills up my spine and makes all the loss of life seem futile."

All that was true. And though the point of his mission had remained consistent from beginning to end, the way he felt about the woman sitting on the seat next to him, the witness he had been hired to give his life to protect, had changed in almost every way. But this didn't seem like the right moment to explain the tumult of emotions pinging around in his brain. Far better to tuck those feelings away somewhere deep in his heart and settle for saying something a bit mundane.

He slid his glance sideways toward her. "Just in case we don't get a chance to talk much after we get to Detroit, I want you to know that you've been the best witness I was ever assigned to protect."

She laughed. "Didn't you tell me before that I was among a chosen few?"

"Still," he said. "It's a compliment."

"I'll take it. And I'll raise you one by saying that you are my favorite marshal."

He grinned. "I will accept your kind assessment as well, especially since it means I'm beating out Ryan."

"Ha. Friends, then?" She reached over and touched his hand, and a spark of electricity shot up his arm and headed straight for his heart.

"Always." His voice was husky as he answered. That concussion he had suffered seemed to be doing funny things to his brain.

After that, there didn't seem to be a whole lot more to say. Well, maybe more accurately, there wasn't all that much more that he was ready to say. He wished that he could tell

Isobel how much she had come to mean to him, how she was the first woman he had allowed to get close to him since Kim. But it was all so complicated, one sad story leading to another. And the goal was to keep his eyes on the goal—getting Isobel to the courtroom it in time to testify.

And before they knew it, they passed a sign for the Detroit city limits. The jagged skyline set against the blue October sky was a familiar sight for both of them, but for Isobel, there had to be pain and heartbreak etched into the landscape as well.

He pulled into a no-parking spot in front of headquarters on Lafayette Boulevard. "In case we need to make a quick getaway back to Ludington. Joking," he added with a wink. "But we do need to proceed with caution until we make it upstairs. The courthouse is in this building as well, so Ricky isn't all that far away from our present location. But first, we check in with my boss and find out what's going on with the trial."

"What's he like? Your boss, I mean."

"Tough. By the book. But most of all, fair. With him at the helm, it's been a pretty tight ship. But expect some hard questions when we roll into the office. Still, we made it this far, so that's something. You ready to do this?" he asked as he opened the car door.

"Not really," Isobel said as she followed him through the sliding-glass door of the building. "I just wish we knew who was behind the raid on the safe house. Do you think they figured it out?"

Jimmy shrugged. "At lot depends on what the experts found at the crime scene. They have crazy-good skills when it comes to figuring out who was shot first and if anyone returned fire. It's just a matter of analyzing the data and sifting through clues."

The man at the security post offered no reaction when Jimmy gave his name and explained the situation. But a moment later, two other guards arrived, their weapons prominently displayed in their gun belts, and escorted them to an elevator that they rode to the fifth floor.

Weaving through a maze of corridors, the group stopped in front of a door at the end of a long, dim hall. No brass plate revealed the name of the occupant. But Jimmy had been here before. Once? Twice? He couldn't remember. Yet the thought of the man waiting for them inside caused a familiar twinge of trepidation.

One of the guards knocked twice, waited for acknowledgment and then led them inside.

"Sir." Jimmy stepped forward, maintaining steady eye contact with the man behind the desk.

US Marshal Merle Miller ran his fingers through his thick mop of gray hair and looked up. "Nice of you to finally drop by, Jimmy. And I see you brought a friend."

"Yes, sir. This is the witness. Isobel Carrolls."

Miller turned his gaze to Isobel. "Nice to meet you, Ms. Carrolls. Sounds like you've had quite an adventure."

"If it wasn't for Jimmy, I wouldn't have made it out alive. He…"

"Thanks, Isobel," Jimmy interrupted. "But before we talk about what happened, we'd appreciate an update on the other marshals."

Miller nodded. "Agents Len Roth and Meredith Strong are dead. Agent Ryan Peterson is in a coma, receiving treatment at Detroit Medical Center, as is Ms. Marsh, who is recovering from a gunshot wound to the shoulder."

Jimmy blinked. How was this possible? If everyone was dead or severely injured, who was the mole? He watched his boss's eyes track toward Isobel. Message received. Further information would not be forthcoming until the civilian was out of the room.

"Ms. Carrolls? I'm going to ask one of my agents to escort you to an office where you can wait to be debriefed."

Isobel returned Miller's firm gaze. "Is there still time for me to testify?"

He shook his head. "The defense rested two hours ago. It's in the hands of the jury now. Sadly, you've arrived here a little too late."

Isobel blew out a long breath as the door swished closed behind her.

So that was that, then. She no longer needed to take the stand. It was what she had wished for in the months before the trial. She ought to be glad. No longer would she need to discuss her marriage in front of a courtroom of people who took salacious interest in her every word. But despite all that, a wearying sort of emptiness surged through her soul as it suddenly seemed that everything leading to this moment had been in vain—the move to the safe house, the murder of the agents protecting her, the frantic chase and eventual escape from Ricky's surrogates.

All that remained was the undeniable realization that she had failed. That Jimmy had failed as well, through no fault of his own. She had seen the look on Merle Miller's face before he'd dismissed her from his office. She didn't know what would be discussed behind closed doors, but she was one hundred percent certain it wasn't going to be good.

At least not for Jimmy.

The elevator arrived and she stepped inside. Sticking close by her side was Deputy Marshal Peter Summers, who had been tasked with escorting her to an office on the second floor. Blond, blue-eyed, looking hardly old enough to have finished college, Peter Summers radiated a puppylike eagerness to succeed at the task.

"How long do you think Jimmy—I mean Agent Flynn—will be in with your boss?" she asked once they reached the small office where she would wait.

"Hard to say, ma'am. My best guess is that it could be a while."

Ma'am. She flinched, recognizing that she must seem haggard and old through the young marshal's eyes. Maybe that was another upside to the fact that she wouldn't be called to testify. She could picture Ricky's satisfied smirk at the sight of her casual attire and unstyled hair. He'd be pleased to point out to his associates how far she had let herself go.

"Can I get you a snack or some coffee from downstairs?"

"Thanks, but I'm good."

"Okay, then. My office is right down the hall. Room 224. Come get me if you need anything." There was pity in Peter Summers's smile as he gently closed the door.

And then there was one.

Frustration pulsed through her senses as she paced across the room. Back and forth. Back and forth. The conversation with Jimmy at the cottage followed by six hours in the car had left her jittery and on edge. And this beige office with its beige table and orange chairs felt like a prison. She needed to do something, anything, to keep herself from fretting about the jury verdict and worrying about Jimmy.

The past few days had taken a toll. The constant danger, the frenetic pace at which they'd had to keep escaping, her worry for Calvin and if he was okay. She suddenly felt like she couldn't breathe. She stood, feeling dizzy, and grasped for the wall. Air. She needed air—now.

She found the stairwell and took the steps two at a time,

taking a moment to compose herself when she reached the ground floor. She had just entered the lobby when she spotted three of Ricky's men, deep in conversation, moving toward her. So far, anyway, they didn't seem to have spotted her. Pulse racing, she made the only move left open to her, slipping through the entryway's sliding doors to the pavement outside.

She took two deep breaths to calm her nerves as the rashness of her actions became clear. She was outside the federal building, with no protection, no money and no phone. Without thinking through the consequences, she had left the security of the federal marshals, and she was completely on her own.

Head down, she quickened the pace, crossing at the roundabout and moving quickly past Fox Theater. This was unfamiliar territory—an area of town she had rarely visited while married to Ricky—so it was a surprise when she looked up and saw the sprawling campus of the Detroit Medical Center.

She couldn't stay in that stuffy office with all her worries. She would visit Ryan. Thank him for risking his life to protect her and Calvin. And pray by his bedside for his complete recovery. She needed to do something useful right now, something other than sit and wait.

She grabbed her Bible from her bag and made a beeline toward reception.

Did they even allow coma patients to have visitors? Particularly ones who weren't related to the patient in any way? She worried she'd be sent away disappointed, but the receptionist didn't even look up as she made a copy of her ID and issued a badge granting access to the third-floor trauma unit.

A few minutes later, Isobel stood in the doorway of

Room 309 and stopped short at the sight of her happy-go-lucky friend, flat on his back and hooked up to a ventilator.

"Hey, Ryan," she said, pulling a chair over to the side of the bed. "You might not recognize my voice, but it's Isobel. From the safe house. Jimmy and I finally made it back to Detroit. But that's a story for later. Right now, Jimmy's at headquarters, probably getting an earful from your boss for not checking in sooner."

She took a breath and continued. "Turns out, we got here too late for me to testify at the trial. You know how I was dreading it, but now I'm not so sure. It feels cowardly not to face Ricky after all the bad things he's done. But it is what it is, I suppose. And we did try to get here on time. At the very least, I can thank you and pray."

She lifted her Bible out of her purse. It had been a while since she read Isaiah 41, but it seemed particularly apt to the circumstances. But before she could find the passage, the door to the room swung open and a tall woman in a light blue hospital robe stepped inside.

"Stephanie?"

"Isobel! I can't believe this. Is it really you? Last I heard, you and Jimmy had fallen off the grid, and no one knew when or where you would surface. I'm glad you made it back, though it's too late for you to testify. My spies at the US Attorney's Office tell me the jury is already deliberating the case."

"I know." Isobel shook her head. "I'm glad to see you, too, Stephanie. They told me you were in the hospital, but I wasn't expecting you to be up and about. You look great."

"My shoulder still feels tender where I got shot. But I have Len to thank for the fact that I'm here today. He took a bullet that was meant for me."

"Odd to think you and Ryan ended up in the same place."

"I know. He doesn't have any family in the area, and neither do I. So I try to stop by for a visit at least once a day. It's good therapy for both of us. But it's a double treat to see you today. Is Jimmy here, too?"

"Just me. Last I saw him, he was in the boss's office at headquarters, discussing the case. I decided to take a walk and ended up at the hospital. I remembered hearing that Ryan was in a coma. So I thought I might visit and pray for him as long as I was here."

Stephanie nodded. "It's a good idea to pray. For Ryan and for me as well, if you don't mind. It's been a rough time for everyone. I'll pull up a seat next to you, if you don't mind the company."

"Of course." Isobel opened her Bible and began to read from Isaiah. "'Fear thou not, for I am with thee; be not dismayed, for I am thy God; I will strengthen thee; yea, I will help thee; yea I will uphold thee with the right hand of my righteousness.'"

Was it her imagination or had Ryan's eyelids fluttered for just a second as she'd read the last line of the verse? She turned a few pages and then began to read from another passage in Isaiah. "'Then shall thy light break forth as the morning, and thine health shall spring forth speedily: and thy righteousness shall go before thee; the glory of the Lord shall be thy rereward.'"

She paused, distracted by a thin piece of clear acrylic stuck between the pages.

"What's that? It looks like a SIM card from a phone." Stephanie reached for the item in Isobel's hand.

The plastic square slipped from Isobel's grasp and fluttered to the floor. Pushing her chair away from the bed, she bent down to retrieve it.

She swept her hand along the floor, finally making contact with the smooth finish of the tiny card, which she quickly clasped in her palm. As she steadied herself against one of the aluminum guards on the hospital bed, she pulled against something soft and yielding—a thin piece of tubing from the ventilator next to Ryan's bed.

SIXTEEN

A wave of blue-scrubs-clad nurses surged in through the doorway, surrounding the patient and pushing everyone and everything to the side.

"Sorry. Sorry. I don't even know how it happened," Isobel stammered. "The tube came loose, but I barely touched it."

"You need to leave here immediately," an older woman snapped as she dug her fingers into Isobel's shoulder and guided her into the hall.

Her cheeks hot with shame, Isobel walked a few feet, stopped and slumped against the wall. "Did I dislodge Ryan's breathing tube?" she asked Stephanie, who had appeared beside her.

Stephanie touched her arm reassuringly. "Don't worry. It was only out for a few seconds. They'll hook it back up, and he'll be fine."

"Really? How can you know that for sure?"

"Isobel. I told you. He's going to be okay. But I'm not so sure about you. You look like you could faint any minute."

"I'm fine." Isobel sniffled.

"I can understand why you're so shaken. It all happened so fast, between you scrambling around on the floor and then the alarm blinking on the monitor and the nurses rushing in. It's kind of intriguing, isn't it?"

"Intriguing?" Not the word she would have chosen to describe a near-fatal incident involving a friend.

"The SIM card, silly. That plastic bit that fell out of your Bible? Did you stick it in there when you changed phones?"

Isobel shook her head as she tucked the plastic bit in the pocket of her pants. "I don't think so."

"We might be able to find out where it came from if we know what's on it. Shall we see if it fits in my phone?"

"Not right now. I think I'd better wait and show it to Jimmy. He had an idea that..." Her voice trailed off as a doctor sprinted past them and disappeared into Ryan's room.

"Oh, no. This looks so serious. I hope Ryan is okay."

"Trust me. I've been around here long enough to understand what constitutes a real emergency. And this isn't one. But go on with what you started to say?"

Isobel hesitated. Jimmy might not like it if she shared his theory about Sam Hunt, even with someone like Stephanie. "Maybe we can talk about it later, when things settle down."

"Okay. But honestly, you do look exhausted. Didn't you walk straight here from the federal building? You're probably dehydrated. There's a pitcher of cold water in my room. It might help if you had something to drink."

Stephanie's cell buzzed with a text. She pulled it from the pocket of her robe and read the message on the screen. "Oh, no," she said. "This isn't the news we were hoping for."

A new wave of panic crested in Isobel's throat. "What news? What's happened now?"

Stephanie shook her head. "The jury just came back with a verdict. Ricky's been acquitted of all charges."

"How is that possible?" Isobel's voice shook with disbelief. "They didn't even get him on the money laundering charge? I thought there was enough evidence to at least get a conviction on that."

"I thought so, too. I'm sorry, Isobel. This is a disappointment for all of us. It's always a travesty when a criminal goes free. But I'm sure the prosecution team will continue to monitor the Bashir enterprise and make sure he doesn't step out of line again."

Step out of line? Ha. That was the least of it. Isobel swallowed hard as bile thick with fear scorched the back of her throat. For the past year, she had placed her hopes on the judicial system. She had been told countless times that her ex-husband would be sent to jail for twenty years to life and that his whole criminal "enterprise," as Stephanie had called it, would collapse without him. Now all of that seemed like a pipe dream, and the consequences of the verdict could not be ignored. At that very moment, Ricky was probably walking out of that courtroom a free man. That meant she would never be safe, and neither would Calvin. Armed with newly confirmed legitimacy, Ricky would be coming for his son.

Stephanie pulled her in for a quick embrace. "Don't fret about this. There's definitely a conversation to be had about what the marshals can do moving forward to ensure your safety. But right now, you need to rest before you keel over right here in the hall."

With her vision blurred by stress and fatigue, it was hard to argue with that. The floor under her feet suddenly seemed unstable, and she allowed herself to be led down the hall. After walking what felt like the length of a city block, they had reached a room slightly larger than Ryan's. Or maybe it just appeared that way, given all of the homey touches. A large vase of irises had been set on a side cabinet, and six colorful get-well cards were opened out on the sill above the bed. Isobel took a seat on a striped armchair as Stephanie filled a glass from a plastic pitcher by the sink.

The first sip of water did little to calm Isobel's pounding heart. But after a second, she did feel better. Maybe Stephanie was right. She had been a bit dehydrated, or perhaps it was just the peace and quiet of a normal hospital room. She looked at Stephanie, who was smiling as she scrolled through the messages on her phone. She seemed far from gutted by the news that her colleagues had just lost an important case. In fact, she looked almost…glad? But no. How could that be possible?

Isobel's gaze returned to the Demi-Deuil Irises on the cabinet. The muted hues of the ceramic vase complemented the yellowish bronze of the delicate flowers. Few people would have recognized the exorbitant cost of such an unusual bouquet.

But Isobel did. Those rare irises were Ricky's blooms of choice. During their marriage, she had been the recipient of many similar arrangements, commemorating birthdays, anniversaries and holidays over the years. Never once did he bring her roses, which he knew were her favorites. Always irises. Rare and expensive. Over the years, she had grown to view them as symbols of her ex's unwillingness to make even the smallest concession to her tastes.

Tension stiffened Isobel's spine as the synapses of her brain made the connection. The bouquet of irises on the cabinet. Stephanie's strange fascination with the SIM card. And then, most telling, her odd reaction to the verdict in the trial.

It all added up to just one thing. Stephanie could very well be the mole who had betrayed the other marshals.

But a well-founded suspicion was one thing. Finding evidence to prove it was another. And the man who had been her protector, her rock, her constant companion of almost a week, was two miles away—with no clue that she was here and no opportunity to advise her on what to do next.

"Isobel?" Having finished reading the messages on her phone, Stephanie moved closer to the spot where Isobel was sitting. She lowered her voice to a conspiratorial whisper. "You seem to have nodded off there for a minute. Are you dizzy? You still seem pretty out of it."

As Stephanie's hot breath coiled against her neck, Isobel flinched, and then, to cover her reaction, forced herself to smile. Forget about gathering evidence. She needed to get out of there—fast. She stood up quickly and began to step backward toward the door. "Thanks for everything. It's been great to rest for a bit, but I really should be on my way. Jimmy will be expecting me."

"Nonsense." Stephanie grabbed her arm to stall her progress. "You're still so pale. You honestly look like you've seen a ghost."

"No. I'm actually feeling much better now that I've had some water." Anxiety fluttered through her senses as Stephanie's gaze remained on the pocket of her pants where she had placed the SIM card. "Maybe I could use your phone to connect with Jimmy."

"Of course. But why bother him, especially if he's in with the boss? I'm going to call a colleague from the US Attorney's Office. I'm sure he'd be glad to give you a ride back to headquarters."

"That isn't necessary," Isobel stammered.

Get out of here! Get out now! a persistent voice inside her screamed. *You're as fast and strong as she is, stronger and faster even, given that she's a patient in the hospital.*

But when she tried to move, her body felt numb and her legs seemed to be cemented to the floor.

"Of course it is." Stephanie tightened her grasp, and with her left hand, opened a drawer and pulled out a larger cell than the one she had been using. Without loosening her grip, she set the phone down, punched in a number and then spoke in a low voice into the receiver.

"Hi, it's me. I have a friend here at the hospital who needs a ride back to the federal building. Can you send a car?...Great...Thanks." She clicked off and turned to Isobel. "It's all arranged. So, sit back down and relax and tell me about your little boy. He must be getting bigger every day. I can't imagine you'd leave him with a cold fish like Jimmy. I do hope he's somewhere safe since I'd really like to meet him someday."

A drawn-out lecture that began with the claim that Jimmy had gotten too involved with the witness had finally wound to a close with the suggestion that it might be a good idea for him to take some time away from the job.

No argument there. It was just what he had been expecting.

And it certainly was true that he had allowed himself to become too close to the woman he had been assigned to protect. He'd made the classic mistake of forgetting his training and ignoring his instincts because... Well, whatever the reason, maybe a break would force him to reassess his priorities.

If he needed proof of that, all he had to do was look across the desk at Marshal Merle Miller. The man continued to frown as Marshal Peter Summers stuck his head in the doorway to say that the witness was no longer in the office where he had left her and was, in fact, nowhere to be found. Following quickly on the heels of that update came even more troubling news: Ricky Bashir had been found not guilty on all charges.

A call from the hospital offered a clue to Isobel's whereabouts. Apparently, there had been an incident involving a female visitor who had accidentally unplugged a patient's ventilator. From the description, the identity of the culprit was quickly discerned.

Marshal Miller was quite suddenly apoplectic.

"Go get her, Flynn." He reached into a drawer and pulled out a cell phone. "And take this just in case. I assume you'll bring her back here immediately. And make sure she knows that she'll still be expected to sit for an interview."

Jimmy was out the door in a flash, headed for the Camaro, which he hoped to find still parked at the curb. He pulled the ticket off the windshield, tossed it onto the passenger seat and took off for the hospital.

The slow pace of the rush-hour traffic cost him precious minutes, but allowed for ample time to consider the conversation that had just taken place at headquarters.

Merle Miller had pushed hard for information about Calvin's whereabouts, and Jimmy had admitted that the little boy had been left with his friends in Madison. In turn, Miller had offered assurances that, since the raid on the safe house, the marshals had been working around the clock to identify the person or persons who betrayed the team. But with the crime scene deliberately corrupted, it remained unclear who had been shot first and whether or not any of the agents had returned fire. But quite by accident, a new lead had recently been uncovered, and the boss claimed to be awaiting final proof before making an arrest.

Apparently, Jimmy would be kept in the dark until that time when the facts would be revealed.

He found a parking space a block from the hospital and headed inside. He used his temporary ID to cut through the red tape at reception and headed toward the elevators. Fifteen minutes had passed since the call about the unplugged ventilator, but when he finally made it to the third-floor trauma unit, he was still hoping to find Isobel sitting by Ryan's side.

Instead, a frowning nurse blocked his pathway through the door. "Mr. Peterson's not entertaining visitors at the moment," she said.

Entertaining visitors. Jimmy's lips twitched at the odd choice of words.

"He's my partner and I was just…" His voice trailed off as sadness and pity surged across his chest. Ryan looked so frail and helpless as he lay there, motionless as a corpse, on a hospital bed. His eyes were closed and his usually ruddy cheeks were as pale as the pillow on which he rested his head. "Oh, man," Jimmy said, taking a step closer to his friend. "I wish I had been able to stick around to help you, buddy." He turned his head to face the nurse. "Will he be okay?"

The woman's voice softened as she seemed to recognize his distress. "The patient did show some signs of coming out of his coma earlier today, so we're hoping for the best."

"I was told that he had a female visitor in the past hour. Twentysomething. Long, dark hair. Do you know if she's still around?"

The nurse smiled. "Which one?"

Jimmy blinked. "There were two?"

"There was an incident earlier involving a young lady fitting that description. She was with a patient who had been airlifted in from Minnesota at the same time as Mr. Peterson."

Stephanie Marsh? It had to be.

"Do you know where either of them went after their visit?"

"One of the nurses overheard one of them mention something about going to the patient's room."

"Could you tell me that room number please?"

The nurse hesitated.

Jimmy reached into his back pocket and pulled out his US Marshal badge. "We do appreciate any and all cooperation in this matter, ma'am."

"Well, then, I suppose that will be okay." With a cursory glance at Jimmy's badge, she tapped some numbers into her phone. A moment later, she found what she was looking for. "She's in Room 384. Go down the hall and take a right."

Jimmy raised his hand in thanks as he backed out the door. Call it instinct. Or just an odd feeling in his gut. But he suddenly had to find Isobel and make sure she was okay. He jogged down the hall, maneuvering past a couple of orderlies pushing a gurney, skidding around the corner and then stopping short as a bank of elevators came into view. The door to the one in the center slowly slid closed, affording only a partial view of a woman inside, her eyes fixed lifelessly straight ahead and fear shading her countenance.

Isobel.

And she wasn't alone.

He opened his mouth to call out to her, but hesitated as terror blanketed his brain. In the moment before the elevator door swished shut, he caught sight of a glint of metal in Stephanie's right hand.

A gun, its barrel pressed against Isobel's side.

SEVENTEEN

A spark of hope flickered within the cloak of despair that had been wrapping tighter and tighter around her chest the moment she had noticed the flowers in Stephanie's room. Jimmy was here. And maybe, just maybe, things weren't quite as bleak as they appeared. She made herself slow her breaths as she whispered a familiar prayer. *Jesus! Please help me.*

She must have spoken her petition out loud because Stephanie suddenly gave a malicious chuckle. "You just don't give up, do you? When are you going to get it into your head that no one can help you now? Ricky has won."

Ricky. At the mention of his name, fear coiled in her gut, snuffing out whatever flash of optimism she had felt at seeing Jimmy. Of course Ricky was going to win. He always won. His network was too big, his web too wide. Jimmy might be there, but what could he do against someone like Ricky?

Please, Jesus! She wasn't even certain what she was praying for. To be saved? That seemed less and less likely. For acceptance? But how could she accept the certainty that Ricky would win? The lack of justice was *not* acceptable. Maybe she was asking God for just a bit more faith? Because even that seemed to be dwindling rapidly.

Why hadn't she run the moment she'd seen the flowers and made the connection? She should have sprinted out the door, screaming for help. There were nurses nearby who would have rushed to her side immediately. Instead, she had stayed, allowing Stephanie to continue the game of cat and mouse. Even after Stephanie had pulled out the pistol, all was not lost. She might have chanced an escape as Stephanie changed out of her hospital gown into leggings and a zip-up sweatshirt. But some sort of fatalist resignation had paralyzed her movements. She couldn't run, even if she'd wanted to.

Of course, there was another explanation for why her legs felt glued to the floor.

Calvin.

Her son was the one thing Ricky wanted more than anything. And now that he was a free man, he would have the legal recourse to sue for visitation rights. Or more likely, he'd bribe some judge for full custody. That meant that she was now completely out of options. And far-fetched though it seemed, her only possible avenue to save her son was a direct appeal. To offer herself in lieu of Calvin.

Ricky would kill her. That seemed inevitable now. But maybe watching her die would be enough. He could have vengeance for his hurt pride, and he could start a new life with Stephanie.

Although the more she thought about it, the more naïve and foolish that seemed. When had Ricky ever taken less than what he wanted? Oh, he'd love to see her plead for pardon. But then he'd do exactly as he desired.

Tears began to leak out of her eyes and down her face as the hopelessness of the situation suddenly washed over her. This was the end. The future she had imagined for her and Calvin, returning to Dagger Lake and settling back into the community that had embraced her, would never be fulfilled. And whatever fleeting dreams she'd had about Jimmy being a part of that future vanished as well. Because the cold hard reality was that her ex-husband was brutal, unemotional and ruthless. And thanks to her foolish decision to visit Ryan at the hospital, she was on her way to meet him again.

"Are you excited to see Ricky?" It was almost as if Stephanie could read her mind as her voice took on an even more cloying tone. "I know he is very anxious to spend some—" Stephanie paused, as if searching for the right word "—quality time with you. He's actually personally driving to pick us up. I thought he'd send one of his men, but I guess he's just been missing me too much. Or maybe he's especially eager to see the wife who ran away from him and tried to keep him from his child."

Isobel attempted to swallow as her heartbeat sped up. She glanced above the door of the elevator where the indicator light announced that they had arrived at the lobby. She considered the chances that someone might notice the gun pressed into her side.

But no. That didn't happen, at least not as far as she could tell. The only possible witness was on the other side of the hall, too far away to see the weapon pressed against her. The rest of the corridor was empty, as was the open space around the elevators that would take them to the parking garage.

Stephanie pushed the button for G2 and yet another empty elevator opened before them. Two floors down and they would reach the bottom level. It made sense. Less people. Fewer opportunities for witnesses.

"I still don't understand how you and Ricky got together." Isobel forced the words through her dry lips. She knew it didn't make any sense, but if she could keep Stephanie talking maybe the elevator ride would last longer.

"Attraction. Pure and simple. We were at a deposition. Our eyes met across the table. After that, it was just a matter of figuring out the best way I could help him win his case. There was no way I was going to let that man go to jail. By the time I came to prep you at the safe house, I knew the defense had more than enough information to put sufficient doubt in the jurors' minds. All we needed to do was bide our time until the trial, knowing that Ricky would be acquitted."

"So, why the raid on the safe house?" Isobel had to ask.

"You were the one who set that in motion when you mentioned Sam Hunt. Before he died, Sam admitted that he had hidden information that would rock Ricky's world. With you being such a good pal of Sam's, Ricky immediately suspected that you might well be complicit in a scheme to gather evidence. He didn't know anything about a SIM card, at least not specifically. But all that exchanging of books and heartfelt chats between you and Sam was enough to raise his suspicions. It just made sense to take you out on the off chance there was information out there yet to be discovered and make a grab for Calvin at the same time. That didn't work, however, and you and Jimmy managed to get away. But your little act of mercy in visiting Ryan offered a solution on a silver plate. SIM card, please."

Stephanie's hand suddenly reached forward and dug into Isobel's pocket. Instinctively, Isobel clamped her own hand against the intruding fingers as Stephanie pried deeper to claim the prize.

"Let go!" Stephanie hissed, jamming the pistol harder against her back.

The pressure was bruising, as was the stark reminder that Isobel could shoot her at any moment. Isobel released her hold and Stephanie palmed the memory card. And something else, too—the license she had used to board the ferry, identifying her as Alice Cullen, with an address of 123 Lois Lane.

"Interesting," Stephanie said. "Just making a wild guess here, but this might just help us find our son. Discovering this little gem has really made my day."

"No!" Isobel screamed, grabbing for the license as the SIM card fluttered from Stephanie's grasp and landed on the elevator floor.

Without missing a beat, Stephanie raised her right foot and crushed it under her shoe.

"Well, that takes care of that." There was a tinge of satisfaction in her voice and a smirk on her lips as she glared at Isobel. "Ricky doesn't like loose ends, so he'll be delighted to hear that's one less problem to deal with later."

Isobel squinted at the crushed piece of plastic on the ground. It was hard to believe that something so small had the potential to bring such an entire criminal enterprise down. Hard to believe that all along, she may have been the one who'd had the proof needed to put Ricky away. But now it was gone. Along with her hope of keeping Calvin's whereabouts a secret.

That meant that the Cullens were in danger as well.

"How can you help that man?" she finally choked out. "He's a monster."

"He's misunderstood. At least by you. I see him for what he is. Bold, daring, rich. He can give me the life I've always wanted."

"How can you say that, after being shot by his men at the safe house?"

From behind her, Isobel could hear Stephanie blow out a long-suffering sigh. "Silly woman. Haven't you figured it out by now? That was all part of the plan. I couldn't very well be the only one who lived through the ambush. Ideally, you would have been killed along with everyone else, leaving Ryan and Jimmy to take the blame."

Isobel squeezed her eyes shut, trying to block out Stephanie's matter-of-fact account of the brutal attack.

"Ricky is so anxious to be reunited with his son," Stephanie continued. "Dear, sweet Calvin, although neither of us have ever liked his name. But that's easy enough to change. I'm thinking Richard Bashir Junior. Ricky's built up such an impressive business, he'll want it to stay in the family. Little Calvin, or should I say Ricky Junior, should bear his father's name if he's going to take over the organization someday."

No! No! No! Isobel wanted to cover her ears to block out those taunting words. This was why she had run away from Ricky all those months ago. To prevent her little boy from becoming a part of that life. But now, with the clarity of hindsight, she realized it was the worst thing she could have done. As ruthless as Ricky was, he had managed to shield her from the rougher side of his "business ventures." Maybe Calvin would have been granted that same consideration if she hadn't run away.

She clenched her fingers into tight fists as the light on the panel blinked to G2. This was it then. In a moment, the door would open and she would have one last chance to escape. She willed her breathing to slow to normal as she flexed her legs. If she took off sprinting toward the stairs, could she make it in time to warn the authorities and save the Cullens?

Long, cold fingers curled around her wrist, anticipating her intentions. "Don't even think about it," Stephanie whispered, her voice thick with malevolence and an unspoken threat.

G2. The elevator doors opened to the sight of a near-empty garage. Isobel had expected to see Ricky parked off to the side, waiting, but the place appeared to be deserted. Stephanie nudged the pistol into her back, urging her forward. They stepped into the glass waiting area.

Still no Ricky.

No Jimmy either.

She hadn't wanted to admit it. Not even to herself. But a part of her had been holding on to the possibility that Jimmy would arrive in time to save her. And she had been holding on to something else as well—a hope she and Jimmy could become more than friends, that they could put aside their trust issues, and, along with Calvin, build a new life together. But she had ruined all that when she decided to leave the safety of the marshals' office. She alone was responsible for the fact that she might never again see him again. The final bubble of hope burst in a wave of grief almost too difficult to bear.

She closed her eyes and thought about Jimmy. It was hard to believe that she had once thought him aloof. Of course, she'd never win any awards for being a good judge of character, so it was hardly a surprise that she'd been wrong about that. Brave, decisive, always kind, Jimmy had done everything in his power to keep her and Calvin out of harm's way. Time after time, he had risked his own life and put her needs ahead of his.

From the very beginning, she had dreaded facing off

with Ricky in the courtroom. But knowing that Jimmy would be with her had sustained her over the last few days. He believed she could do it, assumed she had the same integrity and commitment to the truth that he did, and she had promised herself she wouldn't let him down.

Stephanie's long red fingernails dug into her arm, pulling her back from her reverie into the brutal reality of what was about to happen next.

"C'mon. It's time for the fun part of our time together. Ricky just texted. He's pulling into the garage right now."

Desperation pounded like a drumbeat in the back of his head. He needed to find Isobel while she was still at the hospital; otherwise, it would be too late. Dread's viselike grip clamped hard against his chest as he raced through the first level of the parking garage, peering around columns and into cars, following the only clue available to him. A woman had noticed two women meeting the description of Stephanie and Isobel entering an elevator to the underground lot. First level? Second? It would be on him to find out.

Faster. Faster. Faster.

He raced through a maze of pillars and parked cars on the first level, fueled by adrenaline and a fear that trailed behind him, knowing the danger increased with every minute of delay.

It didn't matter why Isobel had left the safety of the marshals' office to go to the hospital. There was no going back from that, only moving forward. Something must have happened while she was visiting Ryan, and Stephanie Marsh had been forced to reveal herself as the mole. It was also likely that a newly freed Ricky Bashir was involved in all of this, either directly or through his surrogates. Either way, the endgame remained the same.

They wanted Isobel dead.

The terrifying implications and finality of the moment pressed hard against his chest. From the safe house to headquarters, across the upper Midwest, he had done his job and kept the witness safe. But that had all vanished with one bad decision. Why hadn't Isobel stayed put in the room and waited to be interviewed?

This was his fault as well. Wasn't he supposed to be a good judge of human behavior? Like a meteorologist who predicts the weather by reading the signs in the atmosphere, he had been trained to evaluate data, read character and form judgments. He should have known that Isobel would rebel at being cooped up alone in an office, dismissed and rendered useless without any consideration of all she had been through.

But how could he have known that she would wander so far from the safe haven provided by the marshals?

He clung to the possibility of a delay, that Stephanie herself would not harm Isobel, at least not immediately. She'd leave that to Ricky or one of his minions. But before it got to that point, Isobel would be forced to disclose Calvin's whereabouts. And that information would not be easily obtained. She would die before she gave up the location of her son.

Jimmy stopped a moment to catch his breath before moving toward the stairwell to the next level. He thought about saying a prayer then, asking the Lord to help him find Isobel. He had cried out to God to protect her when he was drowning in the lake. Now he was overwhelmed by his own unworthiness in making another such request.

But at this point, it was his only recourse. He whispered

his prayer as he took the stairs two at a time. *Please, God. Keep her safe. Take me as a substitute in her stead.*

If he got out of this alive, he was definitely going to have to up his game when it came to praying. He tucked in a smile, imagining how Isobel would be pleased with his new resolve as he reached the final step and realized there was nowhere else to go. If he didn't find Isobel here, then he'd have to accept the fact that she was gone. And life without her would never be the same.

A sudden realization shook him to his core. He loved her. And he had lost her, through errors in judgment made with the intention of keeping her safe. He had failed to detect the presence of a tracker until it was almost too late. Then later, he was the one who'd insisted on taking the ferry to Muskegon, even after she'd warned him that it was a mistake. He had led her to believe it was crucial that she take the stand and testify, even after he'd begun to suspect that she was a pawn in the prosecution's case.

Above all else, he had broken a cardinal rule of the Marshals Service. He had fallen in love with a witness he had been assigned to protect. It was entirely possible that he would lose his job because of it. But none of that mattered now. He would save Isobel or die trying.

He held the stairwell door to keep it from slamming closed and stepped out into the garage, his ears tuned to any indication that Isobel was nearby. A chill of foreboding shot across his senses as he scanned the row of concrete columns up ahead. There were fewer cars down here, and there was no sign of an active shooter and a hostage anywhere. So, where were Isobel and Stephanie? Had the witness been mistaken about seeing the women entering the elevators to the garage? They might have gotten off at the lobby and were right now headed out the hospital's front door.

He turned and began to retrace his movements just as the sound of a revving engine stopped him short. A moment later, a black Town car appeared at the opening to the ramp and began circling toward a spot farthest from the elevators. As the vehicle approached, two women stepped out from behind a white delivery van. Isobel and Stephanie.

Jimmy pulled in a deep breath. Alone and out of options, he needed God now more than ever to protect the woman he loved. He also needed a gun. But he hadn't taken the time to check out a weapon in his hasty departure from headquarters.

The Town car pulled to a stop and the doors flew open. Three men stepped out, the tallest wearing a navy suit.

Jimmy crept forward, ducking behind vehicles and keeping his head down as he closed the distance between them. Less than five yards from the Town car, he paused next to a beige truck and watched as Ricky Bashir stepped across the tarmac.

"Isobel. We meet at last. I had almost given up on seeing you when you didn't appear in the courtroom. But I'm sorry to say this will be our last time together. My dear Stephanie texted me a snapshot of your license, which gives me a good idea of where you stashed my son. What a terrible mother you are, leaving him with strangers. I'm sure Alice Cullen will agree with me when I visit her later today."

Isobel's horrified scream echoed through the space, a gut-wrenching cry of terror.

"Ricky, no! Please don't do this!"

Ricky scoffed with derision as he pulled a revolver from a holster next to his vest. "Sorry, sweetheart. You and I both knew how this would end. But as I'm a fair man, how about a quick game of Russian roulette?"

He didn't wait for an answer as he slipped a single bullet into the chamber, spun the cylinder and then pressed the barrel against Isobel's head.

EIGHTEEN

It was impossible, but everything seemed to be moving in slow motion and fast forward at the same time. Isobel tensed from the pressure of the barrel of the revolver drilling into her head, watching from the corner of her eye as Ricky's thick finger slowly pulled against the trigger. Tears streamed from her eyes. Not because she was going to die. Not even because Ricky had won. But for Jimmy. And Sam. And Len and Kate. All the people who had sacrificed their lives in pursuit of justice.

The wait was endless. Yet it was over in a flash.

Click. Her body tensed for the explosion. But instead of excruciating pain, she felt herself falling as the weight of a second body slammed her against the concrete floor. She threw out her arms to keep from face-planting, her limbs trembling, her wrists shaking. There she remained on her hands and knees, eyes closed, utter confusion fogging her brain.

What had happened?

Above her, Ricky's voice broke through the haze of bewilderment.

"Marshal Flynn, I presume."

She opened her eyes. Jimmy! He was here!

Rough fingers gripped her shoulders and yanked her off

the ground, and she was pulled backward against the chest of one of Ricky's henchmen, her arms twisted behind her. She forced herself to look at Ricky, who was brushing dust off his otherwise immaculate suit, a twisted smile curled on his lips. Her glance darted to the left as fresh tears leaked down her cheeks. Jimmy had found her. But it was too late.

Jimmy was on his knees, with Ricky's other bodyguard holding a pistol against his temple.

But she couldn't help noticing the determination that seemed to flash in his eyes as he stared at Ricky. If he could find a way, she had no doubt that Jimmy would save her. That's what he'd done for the last four days. Kept her safe. She wished she could speak the words in her heart to tell him how much he had come to mean to her. She had trusted him, and never once had he let her down. Even now, he was here. But it had also been so much more than just his protection that she had come to appreciate. His honor. His goodness. His flashes of dry humor. Her already aching heart felt even heavier as she thought of losing him forever.

"Your dedication to my wife is really quite touching." Ricky's tone held a sneer.

She turned back toward her ex-husband, fear clutching at her throat. Had her glance at Jimmy revealed too much? Had Ricky recognized how deep her feelings were for the marshal?

"Can we just finish this up and go?" A high-pitched voice pierced the silence. Stephanie. She had forgotten the other woman was even there.

"Shut up!" Ricky barked without turning his head, his eyes remaining locked with Jimmy's.

"But, babe—"

"I said shut up. You can wait in the car if you want. But I have some unfinished business with my wife." Ricky finally pulled his gaze away from Jimmy as he slowly turned his head. A shiver ran up Isobel's spine as her eyes clashed with Ricky's.

Hatred. Pure hatred seemed to radiate from his countenance.

The silence that followed was hard to take. Ricky had turned away from them and was facing the car, a cell phone pressed against his ear. She could hear the low rumble of his voice as he spoke into the receiver. She darted her glance once again toward Jimmy. So far, he hadn't uttered a word. Did he feel as defeated as she felt?

No. He looked hopeful. Alert. Poised for action.

Ricky turned back to them, and Isobel quickly pulled her eyes away from Jimmy. But not quickly enough, as a sardonic twist curled Ricky's thin lips.

"Good news about my son. Once again, my lady saves the day." Ricky pulled Stephanie tight against his chest. "My men are just now approaching Madison. They should have my son in—" he flipped his wrist over to look at his gold Rolex "—twenty minutes. And much as I would like for you to witness my joyful reunion, I have to agree with my girlfriend. Let's just finish this up and go. I think I'll do the honors myself. I've already killed one federal agent. And yet, somehow, I think this will be even more satisfying than saying a final goodbye to that traitor Sam Hunt. His betrayal wasn't nearly as personal as that of my ex-wife and her…" He paused for a moment, the sneer returning to his voice. "Protector."

Isobel watched in horror as Ricky unhooked his arm from around Stephanie's waist and raised the revolver, first lining up his shot on her and then shifting toward Jimmy. "I prefer to save the best for last," he said with a malicious chuckle.

Crack!

At the sound of a bullet exploding in the air, Isobel couldn't quell the scream bursting forth from her throat. "No!" she cried as she raised her palms to cover her eyes. She couldn't watch this. She wouldn't watch this.

She pulled her hands away from her face and swiveled her eyes toward Jimmy. He was still on his knees with a gun pressed against his temple. Her gaze traveled upward to the man holding the gun on him, who was wearing a look of surprise.

What? How? Even as her mind formed the questions, her eyes pivoted back to Ricky. But her ex-husband was no longer upright. His body was on the ground, a puddle of dark red blood pooling all around him. Beside him stood Stephanie, screaming like she was being tortured.

The moment felt frozen in time. All Isobel could do was stare down at the body of her ex-husband as Stephanie howled in the background. It seemed like an eternity, but it couldn't have been more than a few seconds before a sudden flurry of activity broke all around them. The shrieking stopped, replaced by the rumble of footsteps as federal agents were suddenly everywhere. Ricky's henchmen were disarmed as Isobel found herself being gently pulled away from the scene.

"Wait!" she said. "Isn't anyone going to tell me what's going on?"

A familiar face suddenly appeared. Jimmy's boss. Merle something.

He turned and nodded in her direction. "We got him," he said. "We got Bashir, though none of us could have anticipated how it would go down. Stephanie Marsh had been on our radar almost from day one. But we lacked solid information to connect her to Bashir. What we didn't anticipate was that you would leave headquarters and go to the hospital. Or that, in the end, Bashir would be part of the mix."

Isobel inhaled and then exhaled. Took a moment to compose her features before saying something she would regret. It would have been helpful to know all that when she was back at headquarters, but clearly, she had been kept solidly out of the loop. "Did Jimmy have a part in all of this?" she asked evenly. "Where is he anyway?"

"He took off after Stephanie, who tried to run after Bashir was shot. Chased her down and read her rights. Didn't you see any of this?"

"No… I…" Isobel shook her head. Her eyes had been closed for most of it. And the rest had been a blur of fear and dread, causing her to shut down and not notice what was happening around her.

"Here he comes now. He can explain it all to you." Jimmy's boss looked eager to rejoin the other marshals at the scene.

"Wait," Isobel called out after him. "Ricky's men are going to kidnap Calvin from our friends' home in Wisconsin. They have the address and are on their way." She could barely breathe as fresh fear coursed through her veins.

"It's okay, Iz." Jimmy was suddenly standing next to her. "The Cullens and Calvin are in protective custody. It's over at last."

Over at last. She had heard similar words before, back in North Dakota, when Ricky was arrested in Dagger Lake. But this time the facts were undeniable. Ricky was dead. His men were in custody. And everyone she loved was safe.

Jimmy paused before entering the airport security line to make sure he had the essentials.

New cell phone. His ticket for the flight to Madison secure in the "wallet." His ID and some cash—not much, but enough to get by.

While he was digging through his pockets for items to put into the bin to be x-rayed, his traveling companion passed through the checkpoint without a hitch. Three days had passed since the gunfight in the parking lot, and Isobel was more than ready to move on. She had proved her mettle during the hours of interviews at headquarters, helping piece together the details of the raid on the safe house and adding her first-hand testimony to the investigation into her ex-husband's death.

But her only focus at the moment was her upcoming reunion with her little boy. The Cullens would bring Calvin with them when they met the plane in Madison, and Isobel would spend a few days with their family to ease the transition from a busy home full of kids to a little apartment where his only playmate would be Bingo the bear.

"I hope he missed me, but not too much," she had proclaimed as arrangements were finalized for the extended visit.

Jimmy's plans hadn't lined up with Isobel's, at least not exactly. Once they landed in Madison, he'd have just enough time to thank the Cullens before hopping on a flight back to Detroit. A plan for what he would do next was still forming in his head.

But in the meantime, he was here, on a plane, sitting next to Isobel. They had already talked in length about the case as details emerged about Ricky's relationship with Stephanie Marsh, as well as the plea deal, which would involve the US attorney testifying against the men who had shot Len and Meredith. And there was much to discuss about what the feds had retrieved from the damaged SIM card, which proved that Sam Hunt was indeed a man of courage who, even while facing certain death, had managed to pass on the information he had gathered about Ricky Bashir.

This was all discussed at great length. And finally, they'd talked about Isobel's return to Dagger Lake. The possibly of Ricky's family seeking retribution had been raised. But all the experts seemed to think that the possibility was remote. His family in Muskegon were claiming ignorance of Ricky's criminal enterprises and seemed to want to avoid further involvement with the police. And Ricky's death had caused his organization to crumble from within. With a vacuum of power at the top, the network had splintered apart, with various henchmen turning on each other. Already two lieutenants were in custody, with the promise of more to follow.

And most important of all, Isobel was eager to return home. She'd had much to say about her future plans, how she hoped to work part-time once she found a trustworthy caregiver for Calvin, and Jimmy listened, interrupting only to say that their friendship had meant so much to him and that he hoped it would continue in the future.

That was the word he used. *Friendship.* Of course, camouflaged in that notion was the hope that, like him, she might want something more.

As they settled back in their seats on the plane, Jimmy turned to face her with a smile. "I suppose I should mention that I don't have a great track record when it comes to goodbyes. I tend to walk off into the sunset and never look back. But I have resolved to try to do better."

"Good to hear." She laughed.

"Yeah. The other night, when I was lying in bed, I realized that I have not felt this calm and contented for as long as I can remember."

She turned to face him with a smile. "We're stuck on a

plane, and we won't be landing for at least an hour. There's plenty of time for a real conversation about why that is."

He smiled at her. "Like I said, I've been in an okay place for a while. More than okay. Lately, I've been really good. It was a hard couple of years after the breakup, but then I found my calling as a marshal…and it led me to you. I suppose I have Kim to thank for stopping us from making a huge mistake."

Isobel pulled in a long breath. "I can't agree with you about that, Jimmy. At least not in the way she went about it. That was an awful thing to do to someone you love."

"That's the thing, Iz. Back in the day, I don't think either of us really understood what love was. Because of what happened to my parents, we were connected by sadness and a desire to remain in the past. It's only been recently that I've come to realize that love involves something more." What had happened in the short time he and Isobel had spent together was nothing like it had been with Kim. He was different now; his time with her had made him a better man.

Show, don't tell. Stephanie's often-repeated mantra, despite her own disingenuousness, was not without merit.

"Did I mention that I started reading the Bible you gave me the other day? It's been slow going, but I'm making good progress for a beginner."

"Jimmy, that's great," Isobel said.

"Yeah. Thanks for giving me the nudge on that. I'm also trying to be a better listener. So, let's talk about you now, okay?"

She laughed. "There's not much to say. I'm in a pretty good place, too, considering everything that happened these past few days. I know I'm going to have to live with the consequences of what Ricky did. Two innocent people are dead. Three, if you count Sam Hunt. And there are probably countless others I don't even know about." She held up her hand to forestall his comment. "I know that I'm not the only one to blame. But just like you, I have a lot of thinking to do in the months ahead. About life. And about love, too."

He took her hand. And this time neither one let go.

Jimmy cleared his throat. "So, where do we go with this thing between us? Is it real?"

He watched her eyes as he waited for her answer. Windows to the soul, right? But whatever Isobel was thinking was hidden beneath those dark lashes as she blinked back tears.

"I don't know for sure. But it feels real to me."

He smiled. "Me, too. I guess we'll just have to trust God and see where the future leads us. A good place, I hope."

She sniffled. "I was expecting you to say that since you live in Detroit and Calvin and I are in North Dakota, there is no way we'd ever be together."

He shook his head. "If you really thought that, then you don't know a thing about me." He cradled her face in his hands and pulled her in for a long kiss, despite being in full view of a number of other passengers on the plane.

NINETEEN

It had taken a little more than a week, but by Friday morning, only one item remained on his to-do list. Still, it had been a busy seven days, beginning with Jimmy's return to headquarters in Detroit, where he negotiated a new job as a consultant, which would allow him to work remotely as part of a team. He was excited about this new opportunity, though disappointed to no longer be working with Ryan. The good news was that his former partner had been moved to a rehabilitation center and was determined to return to active duty.

Once the logistical details were squared away, he'd driven to Ludington and made a few repairs on the Cullen cottage. Next stop was the Muskegon home of Zach Keith, the man who had saved him from drowning. A box of donuts was small recompense for such a good deed, but he was finally able to tell his new friend what had happened on the ferry. Then it was off to Minnesota to return the Camaro, reclaim his watch and pick up his van at the garage that had done the repairs. Finally, he set off to retrieve and return the borrowed canoe.

There had been challenges along the way—some more difficult than others. Hardest was calling home on the anniversary of his parents' death. As the phone was passed among the siblings, he had spoken to his brother for the first time in years. That had taken some grace, so, yeah, *Thank You, God*, for helping with that.

So it was all good, so far, anyway. According to the GPS on his phone, he had fifteen miles to go before he reached Dagger Lake. Isobel was expecting him, so he wouldn't be turning up on her doorstep uninvited.

Looming large in his mind was the issue of their age difference. He was more than a decade older than Isobel, and he worried that she might now see that as a reason for them to stay apart.

But what was that slogan everyone used to say? Expect the worst and hope for the best. And don't forget to pray.

He was getting better at that part every day.

He pulled in a long breath and trained his focus on the road ahead.

For the third time in five minutes, Isobel glanced at her phone. Jimmy had texted earlier to say that he had crossed the border into Fargo and she should expect him around four.

Not to put too fine a point on it, but it was now four thirty, which meant that he was thirty minutes late.

Where was he? She paced the floor like a caged tiger, nerves stretched tight with raw energy. Patience was not proving to be her strong suit these days. Coming home to Dagger Lake had been the answer to her prayers, but it was hard to jump right into her old life after weeks of having her daily routine upended in every conceivable way. And she still hadn't fully processed what had taken place in the hospital parking lot when Ricky was killed. There were moments when she wondered if it had happened at all.

And she did miss Jimmy. A lot. Talking on the phone

every night since they had said goodbye in Madison had provided a temporary balm for the ache in her heart. But it wasn't enough.

She checked the time once again. Quarter to five. Now she was really getting anxious. Jimmy was usually so prompt and reliable. So, what was taking him so long?

And why, after a solid week of sleeping only in short bursts, had Calvin decided that this was a good day to take a three-hour nap? Having him awake would have provided a welcome distraction. As she stepped out onto the balcony and scanned the street below, she considered the likely reasons for Jimmy's delay. Maybe he had gotten lost, or maybe there had been a problem with his van, despite his claims that the repairs had been finished and that it was good as new.

She tucked in a smile as she recalled how amused she had been the first time she'd seen Marshal Flynn standing in front of his vehicle. It was nothing at all like the red Lamborghini Ricky had driven around town, telling anyone who would listen that it was a well-deserved birthday present he had bought for himself. All show and no substance—that was Ricky Bashir.

"Jimmy, where are you?" She had barely spoken the words out loud when there he was, pulling into a space in front of the building. He caught sight of her on the balcony and waved.

"Welcome!" she called down to him. "I'll wait at the top of the stairs."

He must have run all the way because, a moment later, they met in front of her door.

She grinned at the sight of him. He looked the same, but different. The stubble of beard was gone. He was clean-shaven and smiling. More handsome than she remembered, though it hardly seemed possible.

"I missed you." She managed to swallow the lump that had formed in her throat. Why was she crying when she was so happy?

"I missed you, too." He pulled out of their embrace and took a moment to study her tear-streaked face. "Sorry if you were worried. I stopped to get a room at that small motel on Main Street, and the check-in took longer than I expected. I did try to call, but there was no answer."

She down looked at the phone she was still clutching in her hand. "I must have muted the volume when I put Calvin down for his nap."

"How is the little guy?"

"Great. He's cruising now, which sounds like something a teenager would do, but it involves moving around the room, holding on to furniture."

"Impressive," Jimmy said.

"Yeah. You should see him go. It won't be long before he takes his first steps." She smiled up at him. "I'm glad you're here."

"Me, too. Did I say that I missed you?"

"Yeah. We did that already. Maybe we should skip right to the part where you tell me how long you're planning to stay?"

She pulled away a bit more, motioning for Jimmy to sit down on one of the chairs in her small living room. She didn't want to come across as too eager. After all, they were treading into uncharted territory. And was it her imagination, or did Jimmy's face tighten as if he were anxious or dismayed? The air between them suddenly felt tense and electric.

"I'm thinking permanently." Jimmy's voice held a husky

tenor. "Maybe at some point, we could make it official between us. Would that be something you'd be interested in?"

It took a moment for Isobel to register what he was saying. But as his words permeated her understanding, joy and gratitude erupted in her heart. Pulling in a deep breath, she tried to find her voice. "In case you were wondering, that would be a yes."

"Good," he said with a smile, taking a smashed protein bar from his side pocket. "I was thinking you might want this, if only as a memory of all we've been through. Go ahead. Open it up."

Isobel did as he asked, hesitating when she noticed a small item taped to the wrapper. Her fingers trembled as her eyes caught the glint of a diamond.

"It's a ring," Jimmy explained. "You don't have to wear it right away. Everything has happened so fast, and the last thing I want to do is make you feel rushed. But I've done a lot of thinking this past week. Thinking and praying, and I want you to know my intentions from the start. For me, this is forever. I love you. And I cannot wait to become a family with you and Calvin."

She slipped the ring on her finger. "I love you, too."

* * * * *

If you enjoyed this story,
check out more fast-paced suspense titles by
Jaycee Bullard.
Available now from Love Inspired Suspense!
Discover more at LoveInspired.com

Dear Reader,

Those of you who read *Rescue on the Run* may remember meeting Isobel Carrolls, the young teller who ends up giving birth to her little boy in the back room of the bank as her ex-husband, Ricky, plots to kidnap their son. In the last chapter of that book, Ricky is taken into custody, which seemed like the logical end of Isobel's story. But I always knew it was just the beginning.

Just like Isobel, we've all had moments where something has seemed to be too good to be true, but we close our eyes to shut out the truth. Isobel was burdened with guilt for marrying Ricky and turning a blind eye to his criminal enterprise. But it is never too late to correct a wrong. And God never runs out of patience. I hope you enjoyed meeting Isobel again and witnessing her quiet strength and resolute faith in our Lord Jesus.

As always, I love to hear from my readers at JayceeABullard@gmail.com or follow me on Instagram @jceebullard. God bless.

Jaycee Bullard